J 1427924

W9-ATY-349

Christopher, Matt

Prime-time pitcher

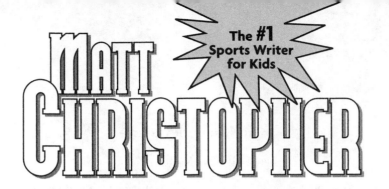

The #1
Sports Writer
for Kids

PRIME-TIME
PITCHER

Little, Brown and Company
Boston   New York   Toronto   London

To Kimberley Marie

First Edition

The characters and events portrayed in this book are fictitious.
Any similarity to real persons, living or dead, is coincidental and
not intended by the author.

Christopher, Matt.
    Prime-time pitcher / Matt Christopher. — 1st ed.
        p.   cm.
    Summary: When Koby Caplin, pitcher for Monticello Middle
School, becomes star of a local TV documentary, he must deal
with the problem of being a celebrity.
    ISBN 0-316-14215-8 (hardcover). — ISBN 0-316-14213-1
(pbk.)
    [1. Baseball — Fiction.   2. Pitchers (Baseball) — Fiction.] I. Title.
PZ7.C458Pt   1998
[Fic] — dc21   97-46394

10 9 8 7 6 5 4 3 2 1

MV-NY

Published simultaneously in Canada by Little, Brown & Company
(Canada) Limited

Printed in the United States of America

Prologue

The Megaphone

Monticello Middle School
April 22

SPORTS SHORTS
by Sara Wilson

I'm taking an upbeat attitude toward the upcoming baseball season. I say this even though the Monticello Cardinals have been putting goose eggs on the scoreboard for more than six years now — way before I came on board the *Megaphone* as your tireless sports scribe.

The Cardinals were once the team to be reckoned with in the Meadowbrook Junior High Conference. Could this be the year that we return as a powerhouse team? Will some on-field heroics finally put some fans in the stands at Cain Park Field?

What will it take to save Coach Tomashiro and our fearsome nine from once again heading down, down, downstairs into the league cellar?

My guess is that this new crop of seventh graders might save us from sweeping up the cinders at the bottom of the league. Just remember the names of pitcher Koby Caplin, battery mate Tug McCue, and their cast of hard throwers, acrobatic fielders, and tough hitters.

Be there Tuesday for the annual preseason Watermelon Game against our arch rivals, the Greenview Green Jackets! It's a home game, so there are no excuses *not* to be there!

Remember — this season is going to be one for the books!

Trust me.

"Sports Shorts" Trivia Question: Who was the first major league player to play all nine positions in one game?

Answer in the next issue of the Megaphone*!*

Pitcher Koby Caplin walked up to the mound at Cain Park Field and turned around to look at the stands. "There were more moths circling my porch light last night than there are fans in the stands!" he yelled to third baseman Billy Trentanelli.

Billy laughed. "We'll just have to let the fans who aren't here know they'll be missing some good ball games if they don't show up. OK, you guys, let's talk it up out here!"

"No problem!" shouted Sandy Siegel, the second baseman. "Hey, batter, batter! Our pitcher's going to be throwing some smoke!"

Koby laughed. Crowd or no crowd, at least he had his team behind him. Not that a big crowd would have bothered him. Koby was used to pitching in front of full stands. Last July and August, when he had hurled for the Evansville Grays in the summer league, he had earned a reputation as a rocket-throwing righty. Big crowds were a common sight at Millikin Field those months.

Not many hitters had luck connecting against one of Koby's fastballs. And if a runner was lucky enough to get on first, he didn't dare try to steal. Most knew that Koby had a lightning-quick pickoff. Besides, if a base runner was able to get the jump on Koby, catcher Tug McCue was likely to peg him out at second.

Koby spied *Megaphone* reporter Sara Wilson in the stands. She was sitting in her customary seat in the third row of the bleachers, scribbling notes in her reporter's notebook.

Wonder what she's writing, Koby thought. Something that will get people here to watch us play, I hope!

A handful of parents were dotted throughout the bleachers, along with some teachers who had stopped for a minute on their way home.

"Helloooo, Ms. Brodsky!" yelled Sandy to their seventh grade science teacher.

"Keep the chatter on the field," Coach Tomashiro ordered. "We're here to play ball."

A small group of Monticello students were sitting on the bleacher seats, an open pizza box at their feet.

"Baseball rules!" yelled one student.

Her friend sitting next to her answered back, "What, are you kidding? Nobody cares about the Cardinals. Just look around you — pizza rules!" They high-fived and laughed.

"With pepperoni!" cheered her friend. Together they made up a "pizza" cheer, to the delight of their other friends. *"P-I-Z-Z-A!* What's that spell? PIZZA!"

Koby couldn't help but hear them. It was clear to him that the students had no interest in the team or the game. Baseball was a big joke to them.

Well, I'll see if I can't change their attitude, he thought with determination.

The annual preseason Watermelon Game was a time-honored tradition in the Meadowbrook Middle School league. Behind the dugouts, each team had huge watermelons stuffed in garbage cans of ice. The winning team would be treated to a watermelon feast by the loser. That in itself was motivation enough for some of the players, for what tasted better after a long, hot ball game than a juicy slice of cold watermelon?

"Play ball!" yelled the umpire.

Under the watchful eye of Coach Tomashiro, or Coach T., as the students called him, the Cardinals took the field. They looked cheerful and bright in their red uniforms with white trim, worn for the first time that day. Their new baseball caps were still gleaming white.

"Let's play heads-up ball out there. Use your noggins!" Coach T. yelled, pointing to the top of his cap. "No mental mistakes!"

Koby, wearing number 33, pounded his mitt and waved to his catcher. Tug waved back with his gloved hand.

At the sight of Tug's mitt, Koby had to smile. In order to catch Koby's speeding, and sometimes jumpy, fastballs, Tug used a specially ordered mitt, the "Hummer." The oversize Hummer was the perfect target for Koby.

"C'mon, Cardinals!" Tug yelled. The Greenview leadoff hitter stepped up to the plate. He had a low batting stance and a high on-base percentage.

"Show him your stuff, Koby!" called Tug.

Thump!

Koby's first pitch was right on the money.

"Steeerike one!" screamed the ump.

Two more pitches, and the batter was left with a count of 1 and 2. He swung at the next pitch and foul-tipped it right into the Hummer.

One out.

Koby got the next batter to hit an easy grounder to Papo Cruz at short. Papo fired the ball to first base for the second out. Then Koby struck out the last batter on three pitches. The side was retired without the Cardinals even breaking a sweat.

Koby walked into a sea of high fives on the bench. Coach Tomashiro gave a stern look. "We haven't even had our ups yet! No time for celebrating — get out there and score some runs!"

Center fielder Beechie Anderson led off with a single, and Karim Omar Watkins, known as K.O., doubled him home. But that was all they could do. Three batters later, the Cardinals ended the inning with a 1–0 lead.

"We need more innings like this one, both at bat

and on the field!" yelled Coach T. "Everyone hustle out there!"

Koby trotted out to the mound and kicked at it with his cleat until the dirt was packed perfectly.

The group of kids in the stands had started to take notice of the action on the field. "Your ice-cold watermelon will be ours!" they called toward the Greenview bench. "W-A-T-E-R-M-E-L-O-N — what's that spell? WATERMELON!"

Koby heard the cries and smiled. That's more like it, he said to himself. A little school spirit at last!

Greenview scattered a few hits in the next innings but didn't cause any damage. The Cardinals were hitting the ball, too, but leaving too many runners stranded. This went against Coach T.'s first rule of baseball: "If you've got runners on base, get 'em home — safely!"

In the top of the fifth, Greenview's speedster Cap Wilinski laid a perfect bunt down the third base line.

Third baseman Billy Trentanelli was playing too far back. He ran in and scooped up the ball barehanded. But his throw to first was off balance and made on the run, and it lagged behind the runner by half a step.

Stepping into the box was Todd Woods. Todd had been threatening to make a solid hit all day. Tug called for time and walked to the mound.

"Here's how you get this guy, Koby. Keep it low and inside, because he always crowds the plate."

"Got it," Koby said.

Cap was taunting Koby with a big lead off first. Koby looked him back and went into his windup. As he released the ball, Cap suddenly took off. But Todd fouled into the backstop.

Cap returned to the bag, then took a lead again.

"Hey, pitcher, pitcher!" he yelled.

The words were barely out of his mouth when Koby hammered the ball to first. Cap dove for the bag, but with one graceful motion, first baseman Tom "the Prez" Jefferson scooped the ball out of the dirt and tagged him on the arm.

"Out!" cried the field ump.

The students and parents gave a cheer. Koby suppressed a smile as he received the ball back from Tom.

Koby took Tug's advice, pitching low and inside to Todd, and struck him out. The next batter flew out to K.O., who was playing shallow in right field.

End of the Greenview threat — for now. The Cardinals couldn't change the scoreboard on their ups. They held on to their pencil-thin lead of 1–0.

In the top of the sixth and last inning, Koby got the first two batters to hit line drives right to Papo Cruz at short. Papo didn't have to move an inch for either of them.

Tiring just a little, Koby worked the next batter to a full count, then walked him.

With the tying run on base and two outs, Koby looked for the next batter. It was Greenview's version of King Kong — Jethro Hubbard — in the on-deck circle.

Jethro had been benched for the first half of the game by the Greenview coach because he had been late to practice the day before.

He was probably busy tearing down tree limbs with his bare hands and eating away the bark in order to make a bat, Koby thought, eyeing the huge seventh grader.

Jethro walked up to the batter's box as if he were

entering a ring for a professional wrestling match. Koby hunched over, left hand on his knee, and shook off Tug's first signal. The second signal was a go. It called for a fast one, down and low.

As Koby let the pitch fly, Jethro kicked his left leg up and swung the bat back. He untangled himself and swung.

Thump!

The ball landed in Tug's oversize mitt. The Hummer cradled it the way a robin's nest cradles an egg.

"Strike one!" yelled the umpire.

Jethro frowned, then looked more determined than ever.

But so did Koby.

Tug relayed the signal, and Koby unleashed a sidearm pitch that caught Jethro completely by surprise. All he could do was watch the pitch whiz by and listen to the umpire cry, "Strike two!"

Next, Tug called for a fastball. Koby threw, but the pitch was a bit high. Swinging with all his might, Jethro smacked the ball farther than any ball had traveled that day.

Koby craned his neck to see where the ball was

heading. *Thunk!* — it landed right on top of Ms. Brodsky's station wagon in the farthest corner of the parking lot near left field.

"Foul ball!" screamed the ump as he tossed a fresh ball to Tug.

Just barely, Koby thought with a sigh of relief. He wiped his brow, then dug his fingernails into the ball. With everything he had, he threw the next pitch down the pipe. Jethro swung hard, obviously looking to punch that ball out of there.

Whoosh!

On the mound, Koby was sure he felt the breeze as Jethro struck out.

The Cardinal bench raced onto the field. Tug ran to the mound and bear-hugged Koby.

"We did it!" he yelled.

"We sure did," said Koby with a huge smile. "We sure did!"

Moments later, Koby and Tug were buried under a pile of cheering teammates.

"*W-A! T-E-R! M-E-L-O-N!*" chanted the Cardinals faithful. "*W-A! T-E-R! M-E-L-O-N!*"

"C'mon, let's eat!" Koby yelled in Tug's ear from under the pileup. "If Scoop gets there before us, there won't be any left!" Scoop Jones, the team's left fielder, was known for his hearty appetite.

"Are you kidding?" Tug yelled back. "They're going to save a piece for the winning pitcher of the Watermelon Game. You're the hero, man!"

"Hey, I couldn't have done it without you and the Hummer!"

"Ah, piece of cake. Or, should I say 'slice of watermelon'?"

The Greenview players and coach dragged their garbage can of watermelons over to the Monticello dugout. "Come join us in the feast," Coach T. yelled to the Green Jackets. "There's plenty for everybody!"

Scoop was the first player in line.

2

The Megaphone

Monticello Middle School
April 29

SPORTS SHORTS
by Sara Wilson

OK, Cardinals fans! I think I've died and gone to heaven — baseball heaven, that is. Watermelon never looked so good as it did after the annual pre-season Watermelon Game, and I don't even *like* watermelon. Too many seeds, but I didn't care if I swallowed them all, because victory sure tasted sweet!

The Cardinals came out on top thanks to Koby Caplin's excellent pitching and the hard work of a team whose thirst for watermelon was bigger than their opponents'. Koby went the distance and scattered four hits with seven whiffs to a 1–0 victory. In the biggest K of the game, Jethro Hubbard did an impressive imitation of a windmill.

While the pitching for the Cardinals was awesome, our offense sputtered a bit. Despite eight solid hits under its belt, our team left several runners stranded on base — a no-no in Coach T.'s playbook.

Here's my take on this year's starting lineup:

1B: Tom Jefferson (a.k.a. "the Prez"): At nearly 5'10", he is a great target for scrambling fielders throwing on the run. The Prez picks balls out of the dirt with ease. Good bat!

2B: Sandy Siegel has the speed and agility to fill the hole between second and first. Can scratch out a clutch single.

SS: Papo Cruz covers short like a gazelle, with effortless grace. A velvet glove and solid bat.

3B: Billy Trentanelli can stand the heat at the hot corner. Sometimes throws wild when on the run. A potential RBI leader.

LF: Scoop Jones has a big appetite for any ball hit his way. Swings big — bat him fifth.

CF: Beechie Anderson has the speed to cover short and back up his teammates in right and left but needs to work on arm strength. Leads off with a high on-base percentage. Base-stealing threat.

RF: Karim Omar Watkins (a.k.a. "K.O."): Right field is the wrong place to hit with K.O. out there. He'll catch anything smacked his way. And you want him at the plate when you're down by a run!

C: Tug McCue is a "catcher's catcher," and Koby is lucky to have him behind the plate. With the Hummer in hand, balls don't get past Tug. His rocket throws to second nab base stealers.

P: Koby Caplin is going to be the main reason Monticello returns to the baseball map! Throws a heater that sizzles. Very dependable bat. You'll be hearing a lot about him this year. He's a player that can bring fans into the seats.

P: Miguel Sanchez: A solid pitcher in the rotation.

P: Peter Chung: If you want to hold on to your lead in the final inning or two, bring in Pete, a dependable relief pitcher.

Want to see how my starting lineup scouting report pans out? Come to Friday's Opening Day game against the Danville Middle School Mudcats!

"Sports Shorts" Trivia Question: What baseball player was a spy for the United States government? Read the answer at the end of my next column.

Answer to the last trivia question: On September 8, 1965, Bert Campaneris played all nine positions in one game.

Koby finished reading the *Megaphone* on his way to social studies class. Mr. Tomashiro stood in the doorway, ushering his students in. Koby had just walked past him when he heard hurried footsteps and a familiar voice.

"Coach T., have you seen Koby yet?" Sara said, sounding breathless.

Coach Tomashiro looked at her over the top of his half-rimmed glasses. "No running in the halls, Sara. But to answer your question . . ." He stepped aside to reveal Koby, who was standing right behind him.

"Great article in the *Megaphone*, Sara!" Koby said enthusiastically. "Thanks for saying those nice things about me and the guys."

"No prob, Kobe. Now I know at least one student reads my column."

"Are you kidding? Everyone in the locker room talks about it!"

"You're just saying that."

"No, really!" he protested. "Maybe you can give us some advice on how to get people into the stands this season."

"Win some games, maybe?" Sara said with a smirk.

"If that's what it takes, I'm all for it. But I was

thinking more along the lines of continuous sports coverage in the *Megaphone*. Then maybe we'll double the crowd that shows up."

"Yeah, to *ten!*"

They laughed so hard that Mr. T. looked up from his desk, where he had been organizing some papers. "Ahem. Don't you two belong in class somewhere? Like here, maybe?"

"Sorry," Sara and Koby said together.

"So how about it?" asked Koby as they hurried to their seats. "Why don't you come cover practice today?"

"I can't. If I don't get my homework and chores done right after school today, my journalism career will be cut short by my parental units. Maybe some other time. Have fun at practice, though."

"Not hardly! It's going to be a tough one!" Koby said. Then they both turned their attention to Mr. Tomashiro, and class began.

Koby was right — Coach Tomashiro was not going to let his players rest on their laurels after the Watermelon Game. He always held tough practices, but the next two days of practice were tougher than usual.

"C'mon, Coach!" Scoop said in a fake whining voice as the team did their warm-up exercises on Thursday. "I'm using muscles that I didn't even know I had!"

Tweeeet!

Coach Tomashiro blew his whistle. "If you practice hard, you play hard!" he answered back. "Everyone works hard. There are no 'prized bears' on this team."

Even though Koby was feeling the same way as Scoop, he had to smile. "Prized bear" was Coach T.'s made-up phrase. It meant that no one was so important to the team that he deserved special treatment or recognition.

Nobody's feeling like a prized bear today, Koby thought. Sweat poured from his forehead as he did his running-in-place drill. But if it takes this kind of hard work for the team to be a winner, he thought, I'll do it.

The team went through its fundamentals drills. Koby threw some easy pitches and a few pitch-outs. Tug torpedoed the ball to Sandy, covering second.

Then everyone took a turn at batting practice. An hour later, the practice ended with five laps around the perimeter of the field.

"OK, Cardinals, get yourselves some rest tonight," Coach T. ordered. "Tomorrow is our first official game, and I don't want to see anyone yawning out there!"

When Koby got home after practice, he went right upstairs to take a shower. On the way, he passed his brother Chuck's room. He peeked in.

Chuck was a freshman at State College now, but six years ago he had played baseball for the Cardinals when he was at Monticello. Sitting on Chuck's top shelf was a trophy he had received from the team, which read:

Chuck Caplin
TEAM SPIRIT AWARD
Monticello Middle School

For the player who,
by his example on and off the field,
demonstrates the value
of team spirit and good sportsmanship

Koby picked up the trophy and stared at it. As always, he found himself missing his brother. Even though there was six years' difference in their ages, Koby and Chuck had always been close. In fact, Koby's love of baseball had come from watching his brother pitch for Monticello. Chuck's team hadn't been very good — Chuck himself had made his share of errors — but as the trophy declared, Chuck's enthusiasm had never flagged.

Team spirit is important, Koby thought. But I want to win some games and make people respect the Cardinals again. Those empty bleachers are going to be filled if it's the last thing I do!

He put the trophy back and closed the door behind him.

3

Opening Day for the Monticello Cardinals was not well attended despite the Watermelon Game victory. The crowd at Cain Park Field had doubled in size, but the stands were still virtually empty.

Since he had been chosen the starting pitcher for Opening Day, Koby was a little disappointed with the turnout.

"Where is everybody?" he said to Tug after warm-ups.

"Well, at least you have one die-hard fan," a new voice cut in. Koby and Tug looked up to see Sara Wilson sitting in the stands directly above the dugout.

"Hey, Sara," Koby greeted her. "Put in some good stuff about us again, OK?"

"Only if you promise to win — deal?"

"Deal!" said Koby with a laugh. Then he picked up his glove and headed out to the mound.

The Danville Middle School Mudcats had been strong contenders for the past few years in the Meadowbrook Conference. Behind their ace pitcher, ninth grader Malcolm Lawrence, the Mudcats were tough opponents.

In fact, Malcolm had out-pitched Koby in a summer league game. Koby was looking to settle that score today.

"Hope you pitch better in the spring than you do in the summer!" Malcolm yelled. "I need the competition!"

Without letting his game face down, Koby toed the pitcher's rubber. A smattering of cheers sounded from the Cardinals faithful.

"Play ball!" yelled the ump as he stood up from dusting home plate.

With a look that could scare the feathers off a chicken, Koby glared at Danville's leadoff hitter, Rock Stampson. Tug signaled for a low fastball.

Koby kicked his left leg high and unleashed a pitch with the velocity of a runaway train.

Thock!

Rock swung hard but only punched a little dribbler down the first base line. Leaving a puff of dust behind him, he dashed toward first.

Prez Jefferson rushed in to scoop up the ball as Koby raced to cover for him. Prez connected with Koby just as Koby stepped on the bag. They beat Rock by half a pace.

"Out!" screamed the ump.

The Cardinals fans applauded and started a "wave" — a very small wave.

"Good hustle!" yelled Coach Tomashiro. "Good heads-up ball!"

Koby got the next batter to ground out to Papo at short and fanned the third to retire the side.

"You're on it, man," Tug said to Koby on the bench.

"Thanks," Koby said with a quick grin. He looked over his shoulder. "You catching all this, Sara?"

Sara saluted with her pencil in reply.

Beechie led off for the Cardinals.

Malcolm looked him over like a bull sizing up a matador in the center of a ring. Beechie had never faced Malcolm, but like everyone else, he knew that Malcolm often threw high brush-back pitches near the Adam's apple.

Beechie stepped into the batter's box.

"OK, Beechie, Beechie, start something up!"

"You got that pitcher's number, Beechie!" The Cardinals chatted it up on the bench.

A fastball crossed Beechie at the numbers.

"Strike one!" called the ump.

Beechie fouled off the next two pitches and was in the hole with an 0–2 count.

"Wait for your pitch!" yelled Coach T.

On the next pitch, Beechie pulled his bat way back but came up with nothing but air.

Malcolm registered his first K.

Next up was Koby, who had been moved up to the number two spot by Coach Tomashiro after the Watermelon Game.

As Malcolm unleashed his first pitch, Koby decided to let it go by. He wanted to see what kind of stuff Malcolm was throwing this game.

"Ball!" yelled the ump.

Suppressing a grin, Koby braced himself for the next pitch. It was high and inside. He met the speeding ball with the meat of the bat and smacked a line drive to short. The Danville shortstop lunged for it but missed. Koby was on base with a solid single.

Malcolm looked a little rattled as he faced K.O. As soon as he began his windup, Koby took two giant steps off the bag. He was thinking *steal.*

Malcolm reached over his head, then quickly switched his feet to attempt the pickoff at first. Koby dove into the bag underneath the first baseman's sweeping tag. He was safe.

"Smooth as silk!" Tug yelled from the bench. "Good reflexes, Kobe!"

The first baseman tossed the ball back to Malcolm, who glared at Koby.

You can't beat me on the mound *or* on the base paths, Malcolm, Koby thought with satisfaction. Summer league was then; this is now!

Malcolm stepped to the top of the pitcher's mound. As soon as he committed his motion to pitch to K.O., Koby took off.

K.O. was an eager batter but let the pitch go by. Danville's catcher, Vishnu Chatterjee, took the ball and leaped up to make the throw to second.

Koby beat it with a textbook slide.

That charged up the Cardinals' bench. "Ooeeee! He pitches, he bats, he steals! It's Super-Kobe!" yelled Scoop.

From his second base vantage point, Koby could see Sara Wilson scribbling furiously in her notebook.

Looks like I could see my name in print tomorrow, he thought. Along with a recap of our victory, I hope!

With one out and Koby at second, K.O. reached for Malcolm's next pitch, fouling it off the backstop. He stepped out of the box to tap the dirt out of his spikes.

He stepped back in, and Malcolm threw a heater down the middle. K.O. walloped the ball into right field for a base hit. Koby raced to third, overrunning it a few steps toward home.

"Hold up at third, Koby!" yelled Coach T. "Good hit, K.O.!"

With runners on first and third, Tug came up to the plate in the cleanup spot.

Malcolm worked him to a full count.

"Come on, Tug, don't leave me stranded!" Koby yelled.

But Tug did. On the next pitch, he reached for an outside pitch that danced away from him. He slowly walked back to the dugout.

"You'll get him next time," Koby called.

Next up was Scoop Jones.

"SCOOP! SCOOP!" chanted the fans. "EAT THOSE PITCHES, SCOOP!"

Koby hoped Scoop would be able to hammer him home and put the Cardinals on the scoreboard first.

Carrying his huge bat on his shoulder, Scoop stepped up to the box.

Koby took a comfortable lead as K.O. challenged Malcolm at first. With two outs, they would be off with the pitch.

Malcolm launched his first pitch — high and inside. It looked tempting, but Scoop checked his swing. Ball one.

"C'mon, Scoop! A little base hit will do!" shouted Koby as he clapped his hands. "You can do it!" The bench took up Koby's chant.

The next pitch kissed the outside corner at the shoulders. Scoop took the bait, and his bat made contact.

Bam!

The ball sailed over the second baseman's head. The center fielder charged the ball on the first bounce. Koby crossed home plate standing up.

"Yes!" Koby hollered. He spun around to watch K.O. land safely at third and Scoop on first.

Malcolm got Prez Jefferson swinging wildly on three straight pitches to end the inning, but the Cardinals had drawn first blood.

Monticello held their 1–0 lead as Koby and Malcolm settled into an intense pitching duel. Koby racked up three more K's, and Malcolm added two to his belt.

By the top of the fifth inning, Koby was cruising with a two-hitter, but tiring. When the Cardinals sweetened their lead with a two-run homer hit by Papo Cruz at the bottom of the inning, he gave a sigh of relief.

Down 3–zip at the start of the sixth and last inning, the Mudcats needed to score some runs.

Vishnu came up to the plate. Koby shook off Tug's signs until he saw one he liked. He kicked his left leg high and threw a low fastball at Vishnu's knees. Even before the umpire's call, he knew the pitch was lousy.

"Ball!"

Three pitches later, Vishnu took his base.

Next up was Malcolm. Koby pitched him a smoker

at the knees. Using a swing like a pro golfer, Malcolm launched the ball over Scoop's head in left field for a stand-up triple, scoring Vishnu. The Mudcats had begun to close the gap.

Billy caught the throw-in from Scoop, then walked the ball over to Koby. "He got lucky," he said. "Blow your best stuff right by this next guy."

Koby tried, but A.J. McGuire hammered a single through short and third. The score now read 3–2.

Tug jogged to the mound and pounded the Hummer. "Right here, Kobe! Show him what you're made of!"

Koby looked at the scoreboard, then at Malcolm's grinning face in the Danville dugout. He took a deep breath.

"You gotta help me wipe that grin off his face," he said fiercely.

"You got it," Tug promised. "I'll give you the target and the signals. You just pitch your best."

Koby did. Carefully following Tug's signals, he struck out the next three batters in thirteen pitches. The game ended with the score still reading 3–2 in favor of the Cardinals.

As the few faithful Monticello fans cheered, the

Cardinals cleared the bench to celebrate with their teammates on the field. When Koby and Tug finally squirmed out from under the pile, they ran right into Sara.

"Phew, what a game!" she said, her eyes dancing with excitement. "You pitched great, Koby!"

"Thanks. But I couldn't have done it without my old pal Tug here. He makes me look good!"

Tug grinned. "And you can put that in your column, with my permission!"

The Megaphone

Monticello Middle School
May 13

SPORTS SHORTS
by Sara Wilson

We're well into the baseball season. Our Cardinals have zero, as in zip, none, and *nada,* in the minus column, and we have four victories on the plus side — thanks in large part to Koby Caplin. Koby stung the Danville Mudcats on Opening Day with his rocket right arm, then racked up another win against the Martin Luther King Mustangs, playing complete games both times. Miguel Sanchez and Peter Chung have worked well together to add the other two victories.

Adding some offensive oomph have been Scoop

Jones, K.O. Watkins, Papo Cruz, Beechie Anderson, and Billy Trentanelli. Dazzling in the field with golden gloves have been Prez Jefferson, Sandy Siegel, and Tug McCue.

Everyone on the team has been playing strong, but how far can this team go? Here's a brief Q&A I did with Coach T. after Monday's victory over the Martin Luther King Mustangs:

Q: What was your prediction for the team after the Watermelon Game victory?
A: I don't make predictions — that's for carnivals and fortune-tellers. I take every game as it comes, as a fresh start. As long as my guys are working hard as a team, I'm happy.
Q: Has the hype about these seventh graders who did so well in summer league met your expectations?
A: I never listen to what people say. All that matters to me is what they do as members of the Cardinals — both on the field and in the classroom.
Q: Have you been happy with the pitching?
A: Well, I'm trying not to smile until the season's over, but I have been pleased. We can always work harder, but we've had some very strong outings from Koby Caplin. Miguel Sanchez has been a proven starter, and Peter Chung has been a very reliable closer.
Q: Any "prized bears" on this squad?
A: If there are, they better not show their furry paws near me. Winning can sometimes bring that out in a player, but it better not on my team.

Q: Thanks for the interview, Coach T. We all wish you the best of luck in the rest of the season.

A: Good teams make their own luck, Sara. But one thing that would help is if the students and Monticello community came out and supported their team. The crowds have been getting bigger each game, but we would like the stands packed for our upcoming home games. Thanks for the interview.

So, folks, you heard it here! There's no game this Friday, and Tuesday's game is away. But try to come support our team if you can! Pitcher Miguel Sanchez would appreciate it, I'm sure. Go, Cardinals!

"Sports Shorts" Trivia Question: Who were the first father and son to play on the same major league baseball team?

Answer to the last trivia question: Moe Berg, a fifteen-year veteran who played with such teams as the Brooklyn Dodgers and Chicago White Sox, was once a spy. He's the only major league baseball player whose baseball card is on display at CIA headquarters.

Without looking up from the newspaper, Koby reached into the bowl of popcorn sitting on the table. His hand came up empty.

"Hey, who finished off the grub?" he asked, looking accusingly at Tug and Sara, who were seated on the opposite side of the table. The three friends had gotten together to do their social studies homework. Koby was taking a break to read the *Megaphone*.

Tug swallowed a big gulp of soda. "Not me," he said innocently. "Musta been Sara."

Sara rolled her eyes. "Oh, yeah? Then why are your fingers covered with salt and butter and mine are clean? The evidence speaks for itself, I think!"

Tug pretended to be amazed at his hands. "Well, how did that stuff get there?" he exclaimed. He reached over and snagged the *Megaphone*. "I'll just use this 'rag' to wipe them clean." He gave Sara an impish grin.

"Give me that!" she cried, grabbing the paper away from him. She smoothed it out and added, "That's the last time I write anything nice about you."

"Ha!" Tug replied. "Seems to me you've been writing mostly about pitching lately. And Koby's name pops up pretty often. You even got Coach T. to mention him. Are you losing your journalistic distance by any chance?"

Sara huffed, "Koby happens to be big news, that's all." She glanced down at her column and looked thoughtful. "In fact, I wonder if maybe I should do an interview with you, Koby, like I did with Coach T. What do you say?"

Tug snorted. "You'll risk being called a prized bear, Koby. Coach T. won't like it."

Sara ignored Tug. "It'll just be a couple of questions, like how you started pitching, who your influences were, things like that. People want to know you better — and I bet it would make more of them come to your games."

Koby pondered for a moment, then turned to Tug. "Maybe I should do it. I mean, if Sara thinks it would fill the stands, then it could be a good idea."

Tug looked unconvinced. "Maybe. But how about a dual interview, you and me, instead of just you? We're a team, remember?" He looked at Sara as if expecting her to refuse.

But Sara just threw up her hands and said, "If it will get Koby to talk, I guess I could include you. Sheesh, what some people will do to see their name in print." She closed her social studies book and opened her notebook. "You two scram for a little while so I can come up with some questions. Go practice pitching or something."

Obediently, Koby and Tug stood up to leave.

"Hey, before you go, microwave me some more popcorn!" Sara added, holding out the empty bowl.

Twenty minutes later, Sara called them back inside.

"OK, ready? Question number one: Koby, how long have you been pitching?"

"I've been pitching for five years, since Little League."

"Have you ever played any other positions?"

"Once. I played outfield for a summer league game when our regular center fielder and his substitute were both on vacation."

"But pitching is where you naturally belong. Anyone can see that. Right?"

Koby shrugged. "It's where I feel I can help my team best, yeah."

Sara consulted her notebook. "Who first got you interested in baseball?"

Before Koby had a chance to reply, Tug interrupted. "Hey, hello there! When are you going to ask *me* a question?"

Sara sighed. "OK, Tug. Tell me, how long have you been Koby's catcher?"

"Oh, brother," Tug groaned.

Koby intervened. "Sara, I think I should point out something you might not know. You see, Tug is really important to how well I pitch during a game. I count on him to know things about the batters and to call pitches that might fool them. Without his steady target, the famous Hummer, I might not be as accurate a pitcher. And besides that, he's great at covering home, throwing runners out at second, and he hits well, too. So —"

Sara held up her hand. "OK, OK, I get the picture. I'll include as much about Tug as I can. No promises, though. Do you still want to do the interview?" She looked at Koby for an answer.

Koby glanced at Tug. "What do you think?"

Tug rolled his eyes. "Yeah, whatever. I hate playing second banana to this guy, but we might as well finish it."

Koby gave him a wry smile. "I promise to remember you when I'm rich and famous, Second Banana. For now, let's get this interview over with." He turned back to Sara. "In answer to your question, my brother, Chuck, was the one who got me interested in baseball, when he pitched for the Cardinals."

"When was that?" Sara asked.

"Six years ago. I don't remember much about his season, only that it wasn't very good. But he kept up his enthusiasm, no matter what. Even got an award for it."

Sara scribbled madly in her notebook. Tug, meanwhile, drummed his fingers on the table. Koby could tell that he had had just about enough of the interview.

Well, he'll feel differently when the article comes out, Koby thought. I'm sure Sara will include that stuff about him. His ego is just bruised now, because Sara is giving me all the attention. But he knows I'm only doing this for the team. Doesn't he?

5

The Megaphone

Monticello Middle School
May 20

SPORTS SHORTS

by Sara Wilson

By now, the name Koby Caplin should be familiar to anyone who's read my column over the past few weeks. Well, I managed to corner him recently to ask him some of the questions I'm sure you've all been wondering about. Here's a quick profile on the player who, thanks to his remarkable performance on the field, has become the standout leader for the Cardinals:

Koby Caplin began pitching five years ago in Little League. He's never played any other position, except one time in summer league when his superior throwing arm was called upon to help out his team in center field. He says his older brother, Chuck, first got him interested in baseball. (Some of you with older brothers who played baseball may remember Chuck, who pitched for the Cardinals during one of their more dismal seasons. I guess we should all be happy Koby didn't follow in his brother's footsteps too closely!)

Always a team player, Koby is quick to point out that the abilities of his battery mate, Tug McCue, whom he affectionately calls his "second banana," help make him look good on the mound. If that's true, then keep up the good work, Second Banana! And that goes for you, too, Koby. Monticello looks to you to keep this team alive!

For those of you who haven't made it to a game yet, be sure to catch Koby and the Cardinals (sounds like a rock group, doesn't it?) at their next home game, versus the Holton Hawks this Friday. (Last Tuesday's game was another victory for the Cardinals, thanks to Miguel Sanchez and Peter Chung.)

"Sports Shorts" Trivia Question: Who scored the millionth run in major league baseball, and when did he do it?

Answer to the last trivia question: Ken Griffey Sr. joined his son, Ken Griffey Jr., in the Seattle Mariners' outfield on August 31, 1990. They were the first father and son to play together.

Koby Caplin had a murderous look in his eyes. With a copy of the *Megaphone* in hand, he strode through the hallways, searching for Sara. Finally, he spotted her.

"Sara!" he thundered, forgetting the rule about no yelling in the halls.

With a startled look on her face, Sara turned to him. Koby thrust the paper under her nose.

"Are you trying to get me in trouble or something? Coach T. is going to flip when he reads this!"

Sara widened her eyes. "Why do you say that? Did I print something that wasn't true?"

Koby sputtered. "Well, no, it's not that, it's just, just — I mean, come on, Sara! You make me sound like a baseball god or something! You barely even mentioned Miguel and Peter, who kept the Cardinals' winning streak alive! And I never called Tug 'second banana' in my life!"

Sara pulled herself upright. "You did, too. In your kitchen when I did the interview. I wouldn't have written it down if you hadn't."

Koby suddenly remembered what she was referring to. He shook his head. "OK, you're right, but it was just that once. It's not like I call him that all the time. And what you said about Chuck, boy —!"

"It's true, isn't it?" Sara insisted. "He did pitch for a dismal team."

Koby sighed, feeling defeated. "Yeah, but you didn't have to print it. It makes it sound like I brought it up." He crumpled the paper and tossed it into a nearby wastebasket. "But the worst thing about the article is it makes me look like a prized bear. I can just hear what the guys are going to say. Especially Tug! You've really made things hard for me, Sara."

He turned and started to walk away. Sara's voice stopped him. "I'm sorry you feel that way, Koby. All I'm doing is giving you and the Cardinals some good press coverage. Exposure breeds popularity. Maybe you'll change your tune when you see those stands filled with fans of yours at the next game. And that's what you want, isn't it? Isn't that why you did the interview?"

She closed her locker and disappeared down the hall.

Koby stood there, thinking about what she'd said.

Sure he wanted to see the stands full. He even liked the idea that they were coming to see him pitch. But he wasn't sure he liked being singled out so conspicuously. And if *he* didn't like it, what would his teammates think?

He shook his head, knowing he had no answer for that question.

There was something different about the crowd at the game with the Holton Hawks. It was SRO — Standing Room Only. As he walked into the dugout, Koby noticed that more than one person in the stands was holding a copy of the *Megaphone*. He glanced at Sara's usual spot. She gave him a knowing wave with her own copy and mouthed the words, "Told you so!"

"They're squeezed in like sardines," said Scoop as he craned his neck from the dugout to get a look at the crowd.

"Does *everything* remind you of food?" Tug asked.

"Hmm. Let me think." Scoop put his chin in his hand and pretended to look thoughtful. "One-word answer for that question, Tug: yes!"

Koby cut into their laughter. "Hey, let's concentrate on the game, OK, guys?" he said. "Tug, how about warming me up? Scoop, you could use some practice out there, too."

Tug raised his eyebrows. "Well, who made you coach of the day?" he asked sarcastically. "Sara Wilson and the *Megaphone*?"

"Very funny," Koby mumbled.

"OK, OK, can't you take a joke? Since when aren't you up for a little pre-game humor?" Tug asked. When Koby didn't reply, Tug grabbed the Hummer and walked to the first base foul territory.

Koby threw a few easy pitches to Tug and then rifled some fastballs.

"Looks like you're more than ready!" Tug yelled to Koby. "Are you serving up any barbecue with that smoke?"

"Barbecue deee-luxe!" Koby drawled with a smile.

"Now that's more like the Koby I know and love!"

Coach Tomashiro's booming voice cut into their conversation. "OK, Cardinals! Back to the bench for a team meeting." The players trotted over. "Now, remember, we're going into this game with a 5–0 record. Pretty impressive, right?"

"Right!" yelled the team together.

"Nope!" Coach Tomashiro said firmly. "This is just another game for us! We're going to be playing as hard as we always do. We have to play every game hard — regardless of our record. Those Hawks are going to try to get their talons into us. Let's leave them hungry! Hands in the middle, now — GO, CARDINALS!"

"GO, CARDINALS!" the team shouted together. Then they took to the field.

As usual, Koby kicked the dirt near the rubber to make the mound perfect. The first Hawk stepped to the plate. Koby kicked high and threw.

Zip!

"Steeriike one!" yelled the ump.

Tug tossed the ball back to Koby. "You're smokin', Kobe! Bar-bee-cue!"

Koby worked the count to 1 and 2, then got the batter out with a called strike three.

One down, and the next two batters made it easy by striking out swinging.

The stands erupted with cheers.

"Listen to that applause!" cried Billy Trentanelli as they trotted in from the field. "Thataboy, Koby! Keep those crowd-pleasing K's coming!"

Koby flashed him a smile. At least Sara's article doesn't seem to have bothered Billy, he thought. In fact, it's almost like he agrees with Sara — that the fans are coming to see me pitch!

At the plate, Beechie was a little too eager and popped out to the shortstop. Batting second, Koby helped himself at the plate with a perfect one-out bunt. The third baseman charged in but couldn't make the play.

With a strong lead off first, Koby toyed with Max Cohen, the Hawks' ace pitcher. Let's see if I can't add a check mark for a steal next to my name, he thought.

But K.O. walked, giving Koby an easy trip to second base. Tug came up to the plate. Max pitched him high and inside, trying to force a grounder to the left side for a potential double play.

Then Koby got his wish. Both he and K.O. were given the green light to steal. They took off with the next pitch. Tug ducked so the Hawks' catcher could make the play.

"SAAAFE!" yelled the umps at second and third.

The Cardinals fans went ballistic.

Tug followed up with a bloop single to fill the bases.

The Hawks' coach walked to the mound and talked with his pitcher. Max was kept in the game — until Scoop ate up his next pitch for a stand-up double, scoring Koby and K.O. The tally: Cardinals 2, Hawks 0. Max was done for the day. The Hawks' relief pitcher stepped in, threw a few practice pitches, then signaled that he was ready to begin.

Prez Jefferson hit a dribbler toward second but was thrown out at first. Then Billy grounded out to cap the inning.

The Cardinals held their 2–0 lead thanks in large part to Koby's rifle right arm. In fact, after four innings, he was throwing a no-hitter, having set down the first twelve batters he faced. With each pitch, the roar from the crowd grew louder.

If Sara's right, Koby thought as he jogged off the mound to the dugout, then people coming to see me are getting their money's worth today!

In the bottom of the fifth, the Cardinals added one more run when the Hawks' third baseman let go with a wild throw on Papo's grounder. Three consecutive singles from Sandy, Beechie, and Koby added two more. The scoreboard now read 5–0.

Entering the top of the sixth, Koby was feeling strong. He wasn't just throwing a no-hitter, but a *perfect* game!

He was feeling so confident, he decided to try something he'd never done before.

When Tug gave him the signal for a ball high and outside, Koby shook it off.

He saw Tug frown, then signal for the same pitch again.

No, Tug, let me choose! Koby thought as he shook off the signal again. Again, Tug flashed the same signal. This time, Koby flat-out ignored him. Instead, he went into his windup and threw a low sidearm pitch. With a mighty swing, the Hawk batter launched it like a rocket at Cape Kennedy.

With his heart in his mouth, Koby watched Beechie run down the ball in deep center and, with a spectacular leap, snag it from over the edge of the fence.

A cheer burst out from the stands.

As Koby wiped his brow, Tug hurried to the mound. "What are you *doing*? You're pitching a no-hitter and you're shaking off my signals? That doesn't make sense. You've got to trust me. I know these batters." Tug looked at Koby sideways. "Or don't you think my job is as important as yours?"

Koby shook his head, embarrassed. "I don't know what I was thinking, Tug. I'm sorry. It must have looked like I was really showing off, didn't it?"

"I don't think anyone else even noticed. You'd have to be a pitcher yourself to catch it. Just don't do it again." Tug handed Koby the ball. "Now get these last two out so we can retire these guys once and for all!"

The next batter took Koby's first two pitches for a 1 and 1 count. On the third pitch, he lined a shot straight up the middle. Koby jumped as if he had springs on his cleats.

Phwap!

He caught the ball — a sure extra-base hit if it had made it to the outfield. He had made a good out and preserved his no-hitter at the same time.

As Koby sized up the next Hawk batter, a thought went through his head: I sure would like to see the word *no-hitter* in Sara's column. I bet my fans would, too!

The eager batter fouled off Koby's first pitch.

Koby's next pitch was a heater that socked into Tug's mitt before the batter could blink an eye. Ahead with an 0 and 2 count, Koby threw a nasty sidearm pitch across the plate. The Hawk batter punched the ball down the left-field line. All eyes at Cain Park Field followed it as it sailed through the sky.

"Foul!" ruled the ump.

Koby heaved a sigh of relief. He dug at the rubber and grabbed the rosin. The crowd was quiet.

Koby went into his motion and hurled his trademark fastball. The batter took the bait.

Whoof!

Nothing but air — strike three!

Perfect game — a no-hitter! Final score: Cardinals 5, Hawks zip.

Tug was the first to reach Koby, but soon the entire team mobbed the pitcher's mound. The crowd exploded, chanting, "KO-BY! KO-BY! KO-BY!"

As the team dispersed, Sara cornered Koby. "Hear those shouts, Koby? What did I tell you? You're the star of this team. You're the reason they're here."

Koby looked into the stands. He was about to reply to Sara when someone caught his eye — a man still sitting in the top of the bleachers. He was furiously writing notes. Suddenly the man glanced up and caught Koby looking at him. To Koby's surprise, the man broke into a huge grin and gave Koby the thumbs-up sign.

Sara turned to see who Koby was looking at.

"Who's that?" she asked.

"I don't know. But he sure seems to know me," Koby said in a puzzled voice.

"Probably just one of your many adoring fans," Sara said. "See, he's even holding a copy of the *Megaphone*!"

Koby shrugged, then headed to the locker room to gather his things.

Still thinking about the man on his way back out, Koby walked by the bleachers. Suddenly he spied something on the ground directly beneath the seat where the man had been. It was a business card with shiny gold type.

Curious, he picked it up and read it:

Dan Marsh

EXECUTIVE PRODUCER OF SPORTS
Channel 5 Evening News

Koby's heart thumped. Television? Why would a guy from TV be watching a middle school baseball game? And why did he look so interested in me? Or was that just my imagination?

He didn't know the answers to any of the questions, but his mind was full as he walked home.

6

At school on Monday morning, kids Koby barely knew thronged to congratulate him on his game. Koby was getting tired of saying "thanks" when he was finally rescued by Sara and Tug. Together they headed down the hall toward Coach Tomashiro's classroom. Standing outside his door, Coach Tomashiro was talking to a man who definitely was not a teacher at MMS.

That man looks very familiar, Koby thought. I know, it's that guy I saw sitting in the bleachers, the one who waved at me! But what's he doing here?

The man handed the coach a piece of paper and headed down the hall. Coach Tomashiro read the paper and grimaced. When he spotted Sara, Koby, and Tug, he folded the paper and put it in his pocket.

"Sara," he said, "I think you might want to come

and cover practice today. I'll be making a special announcement, and I think it's something the *Megaphone* might be interested in."

"I'll be there, Mr. T.," Sara answered in a flash. "And I'm looking forward to watching the game against the Thunder tomorrow," she added, referring to the match scheduled for Tuesday after school. "Miguel Sanchez might not be as exciting to watch as Koby, but he pitches a good game."

"Sara!" Koby exclaimed, embarrassed.

Mr. Tomashiro looked thoughtful. "Yes, that's true. Koby has been playing some excellent ball for the team."

" 'Excellent'? " Sara echoed. "I'd say stellar! This boy is news!" She slapped Koby on the back.

"Yes, well . . ." Coach T. didn't finish his thought. Instead, he stepped into his classroom and held the door open for them. "Once again, I seem to be playing doorman. Why don't you three find your seats so we can begin?"

That afternoon, Coach Tomashiro started practice with his announcement. "OK, Cardinals, listen up," he bellowed as the team gathered around in a semicircle. "The Channel 5 Evening News has decided to do a documentary on middle school athletics. They're calling the program 'High Five.' It will air at the end of the season on a Friday night during prime time. Believe it or not, they've chosen us as the team they want to showcase. We're being highlighted because we're clearly a team heading in an upward spiral —"

"You got that right!" yelled Scoop.

"Yeah!" the rest of the team chorused.

"Quiet! This will bring a lot of attention to our school, and that's why I decided to do it. Now, as you all know, I dislike singling out any one player — this team has no room for prized bears. However, the station wants to follow one player in order to get a real feel for what it's like to be a middle school athlete." He hesitated for a moment, then finished by saying, "The TV station has requested that that player be Koby Caplin."

Koby was stunned.

"Yo, Koby!" shouted Billy.

"He's our man!" yelled the Prez.

"Ko-by! Ko-by!" chanted the team.

Koby was buried in a sea of high fives and friendly punches in the arm.

Just then, a white van with *Channel 5 Evening News* plastered all over it pulled up in the teachers' parking lot. Two men clambered out. One was the man who had been talking with Coach T. earlier in the day.

The players craned their necks to check out the van and the two men. Coach T. gestured to the man Koby recognized. "This is Dan Marsh, sports producer for Channel 5, who will be heading the project," Coach T. said. "Dan, may I introduce you to the Monticello Cardinals?"

"Hey, fellas," Dan greeted the team.

"Yahoo!"

"We're number one!"

"Live with Channel 5!"

When the team cheers had subsided, Dan began to speak. "Thanks for that hearty welcome, guys. As a team, you are accomplishing great things, and you should all be proud of yourselves. We at Channel 5 work like a team as well. We have news anchors, reporters, camerapeople, technicians, and all sorts of people who work to get the evening news out. We run like a well-oiled machine, just like you do. But we feel the best way to get to know the inside workings of your 'machine' is to concentrate on one 'gear.' We've been reading a lot of good things about Koby in your school paper —"

Koby glanced up to the stands where Sara was sitting. She was grinning so widely, Koby thought her face might split open.

"— and that's one reason we chose him. We'll be following him for a few days, maybe a week. We'll be covering a few games, too, so you'll all get a chance to be on TV. All I can say is 'Act natural!' I look forward to learning more about the Monticello Cardinals — for myself and for our viewers."

"Whooeeee!" the team shouted. "We're going to be 'Live on Five!' "

"Koby, could you come up here, please," Dan continued.

As Koby wiggled to get up from the tightly packed players sitting around him, he tripped on Scoop's foot and stumbled right into Tug's lap. "There's our star, acting natural!" Tug quipped.

Koby flushed beet red.

Dan reached out to Koby. "I guess baseball isn't all smooth plays and snazzy moves. Here, let me give you a hand. Meet Buck, my cameraperson. He and I will be the crew. We'll be trying to get that 'day in the life' feel, so we'd like to come by your house tomorrow morning, OK?" Koby shrugged and nodded. "Thanks, guys, and we will definitely be seeing you-all around."

"OK, men, five laps around the outfield!" barked Coach Tomashiro.

The Cardinals jumped to their feet and dashed down the right-field line.

"Hollywood, here I come!" Scoop screeched as he sprinted to catch up with the group. "I hope the camera catches my better side."

"Which side would that be?" Tug yelled as he passed Scoop on the right.

"Very funny! See if I put you in my first movie!"

Koby!" Mrs. Caplin yelled up the stairs the next morning. "The camera crew is here!"

Koby peeked out the window of his bedroom. Sure enough, there was the van, parked in front of his house. His stomach did a giant flip-flop, but he tried to ignore it. With a stretch, he jumped out of bed. Rifling through his closet for something clean to wear, he put on his customary T-shirt and jeans.

Koby went to the bathroom to wash up and comb his sandy, thick hair. As long as he could remember, he was the kid who always needed a haircut. His hair was fighting him a bit today, but Koby finally got it to go the way he wanted.

Well, at least I don't have any new pimples, he said to himself as he looked into the mirror. I wonder if I'll have to wear makeup. Didn't I read somewhere that everyone on TV wears a lot of goop on their faces? Gross!

He gave his hair one more swipe of the comb, then hurried downstairs.

As he rounded the corner into the kitchen, he was hit in the eyes with the spotlight from the camera. Surprised, he fell back a step.

"Whoa! Come on back in here, Koby," Dan Marsh's voice called. "Sorry if you weren't expecting the light. The regular lighting in here isn't strong enough. But we'll click the camera off if you're not feeling ready yet."

Koby saw the light shut off and slowly eased into the room. "I didn't know you'd be filming me eating breakfast, that's all," he said.

"We want you to get used to the camera. Filming you here at home seemed like the best way to do that. But don't worry," Dan soothed. "I know it's hard to be chatty first thing in the morning. You just go about your business as usual, and we'll see how things go. What do you say?"

"OK," Koby agreed uncertainly.

"Great!" Dan enthused. "I'll be sitting here and firing some questions at you. OK?"

"OK," Koby said again.

The light came back on. Koby sat frozen to his seat, trying to remember what his morning routine usually was. He spied his mother near the toaster.

"Uh, good morning," Koby said to his mom. His mother returned his greeting, then walked out of camera range to get the butter. So Koby turned and stared into the camera.

"Cut!" Dan called. The light switched off. "Koby, try not to look right at the camera, OK? Pretend it's not even here. I'll start us off with an easy question or two, OK?"

"Oh, right, gotcha," Koby mumbled.

The light blinked on.

"G'morning, Koby," Dan said with a smile. "We understand that this Friday is the rematch against Greenview, Monticello's arch rivals. Are you worried you'll lose your undefeated team record?"

Koby stared down at his fingertips. "I'm not sure —"

"Hold it," Buck interrupted. "Koby, you've got to keep your head up. I'm just getting hair here, no face."

"Look at me when you answer the questions, Koby," Dan advised. "Let's try it again.

"So tell me, Koby, are you nervous about Friday's game against Greenview? They must be gunning for you, since you're the team to beat. Are you worried you'll lose your undefeated record?"

Koby cleared his throat and looked directly at Dan. "Uh, well, we, um, beat Greenview already, in the, uh, the Watermelon Game before the start of the season. So, I, uh, I bet we can beat them again."

Dan smiled encouragingly, then told Buck to stop filming. "That wasn't bad, Koby. But try not to say 'uh' so much. It makes you sound a little stupid, to tell you the truth. Just talk in nice, clean sentences."

Koby reddened. He was starting to feel a little exasperated. And he hadn't had anything to eat yet. The smell of his mother's toast was making his mouth water. He wondered if he would accidentally spit the next time he said anything.

Dan asked Buck to roll film again. He asked Koby the same question. This time, Koby answered without the 'uh's' and, to his great relief, with no spit. Dan nodded and went on.

"And what about you, personally, Koby? You have a perfect game under your belt. Must feel pretty special, huh?"

"Yeah, it —," Koby started to say, when all of a sudden his stomach rumbled loudly. Buck started to laugh. Dan joined in, and finally even Koby smiled.

"OK, let's get this kid something to eat before we waste any more tape!" Buck said.

Relieved to be out of the spotlight for a bit, Koby got up to make some toast, grab a box of his favorite cereal, and pour himself a glass of juice. As he scooped up his first spoonful of cereal, he met the icy zoom lens of Buck's camera from across the kitchen table.

"Got that drip of milk going down the side of your mouth. That'll add a nice human touch," Buck said. "Basketball players aren't the only ones who dribble." He laughed at his own joke.

Just then the doorbell rang.

Now what? said Koby to himself as he got up to answer the door.

"Sara!" he said with surprise as he stared at her through the screen door. "What the —?"

"I'm here to observe the film crew. Ms. Brodsky thought it might make a good story. And Dan and Buck said they didn't mind if I hung around. Is it OK with you?"

Koby shrugged. How could he argue when his science teacher thought it was a good idea?

Sara took her notebook out of her backpack. She opened it up on the kitchen table, but before she could ask any questions, Dan spoke up.

"OK, Buck, let's get a shot of Sara and Koby together in the kitchen."

As Buck maneuvered into position, the doorbell sounded again.

Koby answered the door.

"Tug? What's going on?"

"What, don't we walk to school together every day?"

"Yeah, but I usually pick *you* up! Your house is on the way to school!"

Tug pushed by Koby. "Hey, is that the film crew? Well, whaddaya know!"

Koby just rolled his eyes.

"Let me get you something to eat," Koby's mom said. "Please, Tug, sit here next to Sara."

"Thanks, Mrs. C. Is that camera on?"

Koby stood awkwardly next to the table, wondering what to do next. His cereal had gone soggy, and he had lost his appetite, anyway.

But Dan Marsh kept peppering him with questions about baseball, his pitching style, and Coach T. and the Cardinals. Koby had no choice but to answer.

"Tell me, Koby, how did you get interested in baseball?" Dan queried.

"My brother, Chuck, played for the Cardinals six years ago. I used to watch him pitch. He always looked like he was having so much fun, I thought I'd give it a try."

"Oh, yes, I remember reading that in the *Megaphone*. Interesting, that despite Chuck's poor showing, you decided to try baseball, too. Who else has had an impact on your playing?"

Out of the corner of his eye, Koby saw Tug waggle his eyebrows and grin hopefully. Koby had to stop himself from rolling his eyes again.

"Well, I guess you could add Tug McCue, the team's catcher, to that list. He and I —"

Koby saw Buck refocus the camera to include Tug in the shot. Tug leaned forward, arms on the table, and pretended to be serious. "Koby Caplin and I go way back. Why, I'll never forget the first time Koby tried out his sidearm delivery. The ball hit the dirt, bounced up, and clipped me in the face. I had a black eye for a week. Soon after that, my mother bought me my world-famous glove, 'the Hummer'!" Tug laughed. "And then there was the time Koby came in so fast to nab a bunt that he fell flat on his face. And the time he threw an overhand fastball with so much force he flipped himself over! Remember that, Koby?"

Koby, now completely flushed with embarrassment, mumbled, "Yeah, those were memorable moments." To himself, he added, Thanks a lot, Tug! Now people will think I'm some sort of baseball clown!

After a few more questions directed at Koby, Dan decided they had enough footage of breakfast. He and Buck gathered their gear and moved to the driveway to get the trio exiting the house.

"For this shot, Koby, I'll be asking you a question from off-screen, so you can look directly at the camera, OK?"

Koby nodded.

"You two go out first," said Sara. "I'm going to stay in the background to do my story. Let Tug be in there with you. We know *he* isn't camera shy!"

Tug laughed, but Koby was silent as he walked out the door and into the spotlight thrown by Buck's camera.

Dan asked from off-camera, "So, tell us about the upcoming game against Greenview, Koby."

Koby gazed into the camera lens and tried not to squint at the light. "Well, I'm a little nervous, I guess," he answered, trying to keep his voice calm and steady, "but if I pitch the way I've been pitching, I should keep Monticello in contention for the Meadowbrook Conference championship."

Buck clicked the camera off and gave Dan the thumbs-up sign.

"OK, you guys, we got what we needed at the house. We'll drive ahead and get ready for some shots at school. See you there!" He and Buck stepped into the van.

"OK!" Koby shouted back as the van took off. As soon as it was out of sight, he turned to Tug. "Jeez, Tug, why'd you have to go and tell him all those stories about me messing up? They make me look like an idiot!"

"Oh, come on, I was just having some fun," Tug

said dismissively. "They weren't that bad. Besides, Dan will probably just edit that stuff out anyway. Those TV shows never show everything that's filmed." He cast a look at Sara. "Newspeople practically always cut out all the interesting parts of interviews. Right, Sara?"

"Sometimes," Sara agreed evenly, ignoring Tug's dig.

Koby sighed. "Well, maybe. But tell me, how did that last bit sound?"

"Well, I could've scripted it a little better," Tug said slowly. "Maybe mentioning the team would have been a good idea, for instance."

"But they're not doing a show on the whole team," Koby argued. "They asked for me because of what I can do on the mound. If they just wanted a representative middle school athlete, they could have settled for anyone from any local team."

"Like me, for instance?" Tug said sarcastically.

"Hey, this gives me a great idea for an article," Sara cut in, eyes sparkling. "Koby, could I get an interview with you about how you feel about being the center of the documentary?"

"What?!" exclaimed Tug. *"Another* interview? He's already full of himself, and now you want to add to that with more press coverage?"

"Tug," Sara explained patiently, "I'm just suggesting it because it would fit in well with the articles I'm doing about the film crew. So what do you say, Koby?"

Koby glared at Tug. "I'd be happy to help you out, Sara. I'm glad *someone* understands and appreciates what's happening here."

"Oh, I *understand*," Tug returned. "I just don't *appreciate* your attitude about it, that's all!"

They walked the rest of the way in silence. When they reached the school's front steps, Tug hurried inside and disappeared into the crowd without another word.

Koby turned to Sara. "That Tug! Never thought he'd be one to get jealous." He shook his head. "Anyway, about that interview. How about if we do it right before the game on Friday? I'll clear it with Coach T."

Sara studied him for a moment, then nodded. Together they walked into the school to start the day.

8

All week long, word buzzed through the halls that Koby Caplin was going to be on TV. Koby couldn't sit down in any class without being mobbed. Lunchtime was the same thing. Only when Dan and Buck pleaded with the students to let Koby "act natural" did the filming go smoothly.

Yet even then, everything wasn't one hundred percent normal. By Thursday, Tug had stopped walking to school with Koby. At first Koby tried to draw Tug back into the picture. But with school, practice, and the film, Koby had hardly any free time for that.

Finally it was Friday, the day of the rematch against Greenview.

At the start of school, the film crew set up near

the trophy case in the front hall. When Koby and Sara arrived, they hurried Koby into the spotlight. Dan started firing questions at Koby. Koby, used to the lights and do's and don'ts of filming by now, settled in to answer them. All the while, the audience around him grew bigger and bigger.

"And this is how I hold my fastball. I grip the ball like this," Koby said, holding up his hand with a pretend ball in it. "Then I snap my wrist right before the release to get the ultimate velocity with my pitch."

Mr. Tomashiro appeared outside his classroom door. He approached the film crew.

"Excuse me," he said in his best "trying to keep cool" voice. The students opened a path. "Homeroom is starting now. Koby, come along."

"OK, Coach T.," Koby said. He glanced back into the camera. "You need to be sure that your grip on the ball is —"

"Now!" ordered Mr. Tomashiro. Buck and Dan helped to disperse the crowd.

"OK, folks," Dan said as he gently nudged the students to move. "Time to get to class."

"Well, gotta go!" Koby said. Looking into the still-running camera one more time, he added, "School comes first! You have to study hard and take that discipline with you onto the field."

As the camera shut off, Koby thought he saw one student mouth to another, "Oh, brother." But he wasn't sure.

Mr. T. followed Koby into homeroom, with Dan and Buck close behind. Koby saw Buck click on the camera and point it at Mr. Tomashiro. Mr. T. didn't appear to notice.

"Here are today's announcements. Retakes for class pictures will be today and Monday. All signed permission slips for the seventh grade overnight camping trip to Sander's Pond must be handed in to me by Monday or you won't be able to go. And, as you all must know, or hopefully know, today is the big rematch against the Greenview Green Jackets. We had a great crowd at our last home game. Let's see if we can even do better with today's crowd. It's going to be a good game. See you there at three."

"Uh, Coach T., could I add a few words?" Koby stood up.

Coach Tomashiro's eyebrows shot up, but he nodded.

"I'll be on the mound today for the Cardinals,"

Koby said, "and let me just say how much I've appreciated everyone's support so far this season. It really helps me to hear you yelling my name. So come on out and keep up the good work!"

When Koby's impromptu speech was over, Mr. Tomashiro dismissed the class to their first period.

Dan and Buck gathered their gear and followed Koby into the mad rush in the halls. Koby spotted a familiar figure up ahead of him.

On impulse, he cried, "Hey, there's Tug! Catch this shot!"

Koby ran up to Tug and drew him into camera range before Tug could protest. With his arm around him, Koby said in his best cheery voice, "Tug McCue has a tough job, catching my fireballs. He even has to use a special oversize mitt in order to soften the blow!"

Tug frowned slightly, but he recovered fast. "Yeah, and it comes in handy for fielding Koby's wild pitches, too."

Buck and Dan laughed, and Buck cut filming. When they were out of earshot, Koby pulled back from Tug. "Why'd you say that?" he demanded.

Tug shrugged. "It's true. Your pitches are wild

sometimes. Besides, it's not any worse than what you said about me. Made it sound like I needed a glove as thick as a mattress to catch your heat without hurting myself!"

"Well, don't you?" Koby started to retort.

Dan interrupted before the argument could escalate any further. "Well, we have enough school shots for now. We'll see you on the field for the game this afternoon."

Koby followed them a few paces down the hall. "You don't use everything you film for the documentary, do you?" he asked anxiously.

Dan and Buck exchanged glances. "No," said Dan. "Only the stuff that seems relevant. In this case, only stuff that helps viewers understand what middle school athletics are all about."

Koby wasn't sure that that answered the question he had meant to ask, but Dan and Buck left before he could think how to pose the query again. And when he looked for Tug, Tug had disappeared.

That afternoon before the game, Koby found Sara standing outside the locker room. She was carrying her notebook and pencil.

"Hi, Sara. Shouldn't you be hurrying to get your favorite seat at the game?" Koby asked with a smile.

Sara frowned. "Koby, you're supposed to give me an interview today, remember? We talked about it earlier this week and you said —"

Koby smacked his hand to his forehead. "Oh yeah! Hold on. I just have to go in and tell Coach T. I'm going to be a few minutes late for warm-ups," he said.

He slipped into the locker room and looked for the coach. But he couldn't find him anywhere. With a shrug, he reached for the door handle to tell Sara, when the sound of voices made him pause.

"Hey, Tug, why aren't you in there getting ready?" he heard Sara say.

"I was doing an errand for Principal Sleeper. He wanted someone to help the school nurse put away some big boxes of medical supplies. What's up? What're you doing here?"

"I'm supposed to do an interview with Koby. Of course, Mr. Hotshot forgot, so now he's in there clearing it with Coach T."

Tug snorted. "The way he's been this week, I'm

not sure I'd be able to handle hearing Koby talk about himself."

Sara laughed. "Yeah, I know what you mean. But I already told Ms. Brodsky I'd do it, so the *Megaphone* is holding a space for it. I can't wiggle out of it."

"Good luck. Try not to throw up if you can!"

Tug's voice got louder, and Koby guessed he was about to come into the locker room. Koby ducked behind a row of lockers until he heard Tug go by.

That rat! he thought angrily. And Sara, too! I don't know if I even want to do the interview now!

He debated what to do for a few moments, then decided he would do the interview after all. He still hadn't found Coach T., but figured he'd just give Sara five minutes. He'd be at warm-ups before he was missed, he was sure.

He stepped out of the locker room. Sara pointed to some benches and suggested they sit there.

"You did clear this with Coach T., right?" she asked before they began.

"Yes, he said it was fine," Koby fibbed. "So what do you want me to talk about? What it's like to be in front of the camera, or to be followed around all day by a film crew, or to be mobbed by kids I don't even know?"

Before Sara could reply, someone behind them cleared his throat. Koby spun around and saw Coach Tomashiro standing by the locker room door, arms folded over his chest.

"Excuse me, Sara, Koby. Koby, aren't you supposed to be doing something right now?"

"Uh, Coach T., I tried to find you. Sara wants to do another piece on me for the *Megaphone*, see, and —"

Sara cut in. "Wait a minute. You just told me Coach T. had given you permission to be late for warm-ups. Were you lying to me or something?"

Koby, flustered, tried to explain. But he gave up when he saw the fury in Sara's eyes.

"I'm sorry." He stood up. "Coach, I'll get right out to the field and start warming up."

"Yes, I think that's a fine idea." Coach T.'s voice was steely. "You know, Koby, it's stunts like that that bench starting players." Koby felt his heart lunge into his throat. "However, given the circumstances," Coach T. continued, "I suppose I can't do that. But before you go, Koby, isn't there something you would like to say?"

Koby turned back to Sara, but couldn't meet her eyes. "Sorry, Sara. Uh, if you still want to do the interview, how about I meet you here after the game and we do it then?"

"You know what? Just forget it. I'll give a longer report on today's game instead," Sara said curtly.

"OK, Koby. Inside and into uniform."

Just as Coach T. opened the door to go back into the locker room, Tug came out, dressed for the game. He greeted Coach T., who nodded and continued inside. Tug passed Koby without a word.

"Pretty quick interview, Sara," Tug observed in a voice loud enough for Koby to hear.

"It was over before it began!" Sara spat. "That Koby really is starting to get on my nerves! What's it going to take to bring him back to reality?"

Cain Park Field was at its best when it was SRO. The creaky bleachers didn't creak as much when the stands were full.

This afternoon, there was extra excitement, caused by Dan Marsh and his cameraman, Buck. All week, players had been told to get out of camera range during Dan's interviews with Koby. Now they'd have their chance to shine in their own light.

Coach Tomashiro tried to rein in his boisterous team. "OK, you guys, forget the cameras for a minute and listen up. We've got a game to play, and the Green Jackets are going to be ready. Are *you* ready?"

"Ready!" the team yelled in unison.

"Then let's get out there and play some ball.

Camera crew, you'll have to stand way back in foul territory behind the dugout, OK?"

Dan and Buck gave Coach T. the "no prob" thumbs-up.

The coach called Koby aside. "I hope you're ready to concentrate on your pitching and not the camera, Koby. Just know that if at any time I feel you're not giving this game your all, I'm sending Peter in to relieve you — documentary or no documentary. Understand?"

Koby nodded silently.

"OK, good. Now, get in there and pitch the game I know you're capable of!"

"Batter up!" yelled the ump.

Tug walked up to Koby and placed the ball in his hands. "Think you can forget about the cameras and pitch a game?" he said tightly.

Koby took the ball without saying a word and tugged at the brim of his cap. Why is everybody getting on me about the cameras? he wondered. Sheesh, you'd think I couldn't handle being in the spotlight or something! Well, I'll show them.

Koby mowed down the first two batters he faced. The crowd cheered lustily.

When Todd Woods came up to the plate, Koby had some trouble finding the strike zone. Todd crowded the plate and stayed in there with a 3–1 count.

Then Koby threw a low ball in the dirt that got by Tug. "Settle down," yelled Tug as the ball bounced to the backstop and Todd took his base.

Batting cleanup was Jethro Hubbard.

Koby crouched over and put his gloved hand on his left knee. As he stared down Jethro, a movement registered out of the corner of his eye. Shifting his gaze slightly, he saw Todd increasing his lead off first base by two steps. Todd looked ready to fly. Prez Jefferson casually walked to the bag and firmly placed his right heel on the corner.

Koby spun and threw in a motion faster than a fly flapping its wings.

Prez had his glove on the bag, and the ball zoomed right into it, beating Todd's outstretched hand by two feet. Once the fans realized what had happened, they roared with approval.

"Thataboy, Kobe!" Prez shouted to Koby as they trotted back to the dugout together. Koby acknowledged him with a tip of his cap.

It was the Cardinals' turn to see what they could do at the plate. Beechie led off with a short hopper to second for a routine out.

Koby stepped up to the plate. His eye caught a gleam of sunlight off Buck's camera lens.

Suddenly, for the first time since the spotlight had hit him in his kitchen, he was nervous about being in front of the camera.

What if I strike out? he thought wildly.

He stood outside the batter's box for a few seconds, trying to relax his hands as they white-knuckled the bat. When he finally stepped in, he ended up looking at the first five pitches without swinging, running the count to 3–2.

Come on, Koby, he thought, trying to psyche himself up. You've got to swing at the next one.

He did. But he fouled it off. He fouled off the next pitch, too, and then hit a weak grounder back to the pitcher for easy out number two.

He walked despondently back to the dugout, got himself a cup of water, then took the only seat available — an open spot next to Tug. He half hoped the catcher would give him an encouraging word. But Tug just looked at him and said, "Too bad. Wonder if they'll keep that in your precious documentary."

Koby didn't have time to reply because the next batter got out. So, without a word to Tug, Koby grabbed his glove and stalked out to the field.

Jealousy, that's all it is, he thought. Well, if that's the way he wants to play things, I can sure do that.

In the top of the second, Jethro walked up to the plate like a broncobuster about to ride the meanest, wildest mustang in the West.

Tug called for a sidearm pitch to hit high and outside. But Koby, still smarting from Tug's biting comment, decided to do things differently. Very differently.

He ignored the signal and threw an overarm fastball that screamed toward the plate. It looked like a strike until it curved sharply at the last moment. Tug had to move quickly to capture it.

"Ball!" the umpire yelled.

Tug hurled the ball back with such force that it stung Koby's gloved hand. The pain just fueled Koby's temper. He had been planning to follow Tug's signal this time. But instead, he ignored him on the next two pitches — and got behind in the count, 3–0.

Tug called for time. "What're you doing, man?" he asked furiously when he reached the mound.

"I'm calling the pitches myself, that's what. All good pitchers do."

"Oh, yeah? Well, maybe *their* catchers don't mind not knowing what the pitcher is going to throw at them, but I do. Besides, I know these batters! Now, let me call the pitches, would you?"

"I know what I'm doing," Koby said stubbornly.

"C'mon, play ball!" screamed the ump from behind home plate. Tug shot Koby one last angry look, then trotted back to his position. He didn't even bother to signal this time. He just held up the Hummer and waited.

Now, that's more like it, Koby thought, trying to feel satisfied. He reared back and let loose with a fastball.

Jethro connected for a towering pop fly deep into right. Luckily, K.O. got a good jump on it and made a hard play look easy. One out.

Despite Jethro's solid connection, Koby continued to call his own pitches. Tug didn't signal once.

The batters made a few hits, but Beechie and Billy handled them and the side went down without scoring a run.

The Greenview pitcher struggled in the bottom of the second. With one out, he walked Scoop, then Prez singled, and Billy hit an RBI double that sent Scoop home and Prez to third. The Cardinals were first on the scoreboard but couldn't add to their lead that time at bat.

The third inning was uneventful for both sides. Taking his 1–0 lead into the fourth, Koby unleashed two solid fastballs, then a sidearm pitch for a third strike on the first batter. But the last pitch skipped past Tug to the backstop.

Oh, no! Koby's mind screamed. Tug scrambled for the ball but, per the "drop-third-strike rule," the batter took off for first and beat Tug's throw by half a step.

Tug was charged with the error. As he returned to his position, he slapped the Hummer hard against his thigh.

A twang of guilt tugged at Koby. *If you had let Tug call the pitch,* a little voice inside him murmured, *he would have been prepared for the* sidearm, and maybe the ball wouldn't have gotten away from him.

Koby shook himself. Tug should be prepared for all my pitches, he argued silently. That's why the error was charged to him, not me.

But for some reason, Koby couldn't judge which pitch to throw to which batter after that. Cap Wilinski hit a long fly ball deep into left that Scoop couldn't get to in time. Cap stood up grinning on second.

No outs, runner on second.

"OK, you guys, play it hard! You can do it!" yelled Coach Tomashiro from the sidelines.

Koby reared back and threw a fastball. The Greenview batter clobbered it toward Beechie in center. Beechie misjudged it, allowing the ball to sail over his head for an RBI double. Cap Wilinski was greeted by cheers from his teammates as he crossed the plate, tying the game up at 1–1. The next batter took the sacrifice, advancing the runner to third. Next up was Jethro. He hit a hard grounder to short. Papo stopped it with a dive down on one knee. Papo held the runner at third, then made the play to first for the second out.

With two down, a lefty batter hit a full-count pitch that bounced through Billy's legs at third. Another run scored. Koby glared at Billy as Billy smoothed out the dirt where the ball had taken its fatal bounce.

Koby finally finished off the inning with a strike-out, but the damage had been done. Greenview 2, Monticello 1.

That's the way the score stayed until the fifth inning.

With one out, Cap Wilinski sliced a ball between first and second that Sandy got a piece of but couldn't get a handle on. Cap advanced on Jethro's sacrifice.

The next batter smacked a one-hopper to Sandy, who fumbled again. Sandy made a late throw to Prez, putting runners on first and third. A fly ball to K.O. advanced the runners, and another run scored. Koby got out of the team tailspin by relying on his fastball and striking out the final batter. Green Jackets 3, Cardinals 1.

The Cardinals' bats remained mute. Koby bet they couldn't hit the broad side of a barn, no matter how hard they tried. They went into the last inning still down by two runs.

Greenview threatened when Papo overthrew to Prez at first.

Jeez, is this whole team falling apart? Koby thought disgustedly. Who hasn't made an error today? And they talk about me getting camera jitters.

He tried not to think about the number of hits Greenview had scored off him, nor the number of balls he had thrown. Compared to the previous games, those numbers were much higher than usual.

In the final Greenview at bat, Koby struck out two and forced a ground-out.

But the Cardinals couldn't rise to the occasion as the top of the order — Beechie, Koby, and K.O. — went down 1-2-3. Final score: Greenview 3, Monticello 1.

As the Cardinals gathered up their gear, Koby couldn't contain his frustration. "Well, that game sure is going to look lousy on film," he sneered as Tug passed him, lugging his catcher's equipment.

"I thought our goal was to play our hardest as a team, not look good for your big prime-time debut!" Tug shot back. "And by the way, I can't say that you were looking that good yourself. But, hey, forget teamwork. Forget your friends."

Koby's frustration was fueled by the anger in Tug's voice. "Yeah, well, maybe I will!"

Koby glanced up — and balked when he saw Buck and Dan standing there. Buck's camera was still rolling.

Koby turned away, and saw Sara talking with Tug. As he watched, she shook her head and jotted something in her notebook, then gathered her belongings and left without a backward glance.

That's when Koby noticed the last person sitting in the stands. The person stood up and walked down the bleachers toward Koby with his hand out-stretched and a mile-wide smile on his face. When Koby saw who it was, his jaw dropped.

Chuck!" Koby yelled.

"Hey, little brother! Quite a surprise, huh?" Chuck said as he gave Koby a big bear hug.

"I'll say! What are you doing here?"

"I got a call from Mom because the Channel 5 guys wanted to film a brief segment with you and me together. You know, sort of a 'how the medium-good older brother athlete inspired his superstar brother' kind of thing."

"Cut it out, man! You were the best!"

"Well, I did have a lot of fun hanging with my Cardinal buddies, that's for sure." He looked around as if he expected to see a crowd of Koby's teammates surrounding Koby, too. "Anyway, I wish my college was closer so I could catch more of your games, but being almost a three-hour drive away makes it tough."

"I know, but you're here now, and that's great!"

"The pleasure is all mine, little brother. Mom and Dad have been telling me how you've been tearing up the Meadowbrook Conference. Must have been all those games of catch we played in the driveway."

"Not hardly!" Koby said with a big laugh. "I think it's from eating the famous triple-decker peanut butter and marshmallow sandwiches you taught me to make!"

"Ugh, do you still eat those?" Chuck groaned, holding his stomach. "Great food for an athlete! Now, come on, let's get home. I understand the camera crew is going to show up, and I'm sure you want to get a shower so you can be all pretty for them!"

An hour later, Koby was clean and dressed in his best casual clothes.

"Boys, Dan and Buck are here!" Koby's mom yelled from the downstairs hallway. "I'm sending them up!"

"OK, Mom!" Koby yelled back as he and Chuck

headed to the hallway at the top of the stairs. "Come on up, you guys!"

Dan and Buck walked up the stairs. Koby introduced them to Chuck.

"Thanks for throwing this opportunity to Koby," Chuck said. "I bet he's enjoying all the attention and being filmed by you guys."

"I don't think we're going to win an Oscar, but we sure are learning a lot about middle school athletics," Buck answered. "Hopefully we'll get some good stuff tonight that we can use for our promo ads. Those are going to start to run soon. The documentary is scheduled to air on Friday of the week after the last game, against Runkle."

"Cool," Koby said, beaming.

Koby started to lead them down the narrow hallway to his room. Dan peeked into the open doorway of Chuck's room.

"This must be your room, right, Chuck?" asked Dan. "Forgive me for nosing my head in there."

"That's OK," said Chuck. "Although I think it's been cleaned up a bit since I've been away at school. I can't find my favorite dirty T-shirts hidden under the bed anymore!"

Dan chuckled.

"Mind if we start in here with the trophy shelf in the background?" Dan asked.

"Go right ahead," Chuck said. "I'm pretty proud of what's up there."

"Sounds good to me," Koby said, trying to get a word in.

"Great, then let's get started. Buck, get a shot of the trophy case, OK? Then if you two will sit here, we can get the best angle," Dan said as he directed Buck where to set up.

Koby and Chuck sat down and stared directly into the camera.

"Hey, relax, you guys. It looks like you're sitting on a bed of nails!" Dan said.

Koby and Chuck grinned at each other.

"Good, now that you're smiling a bit for the camera, we can get started. Chuck, let's begin with you. I know that you also played for Monticello. What was the most memorable thing about playing for MMS, if you can think that far back?" Dan asked with a twinkle in his eye.

"Now, wait a sec," Chuck protested. "It wasn't *that* far back! But, to answer your question, I do remember one thing above everything else. It was getting this award."

Chuck turned around and picked up his team spirit trophy. Holding it proudly, he said, "This trophy, given for demonstrating the most team spirit, meant a lot to me. It was a great honor to get. Now, I certainly wasn't the greatest player — you can ask Coach T. about that — but I gave it all I had. That's what it was all about for me."

The camera zoomed in on the trophy and then closed in on Koby's face as he watched and listened to Chuck talk.

"How much of an influence has your brother been on your ball playing?" Dan asked Koby.

"A lot! I remember watching him play at MMS when I was a little kid. They sure didn't win many games, and —"

"You can say that again!" Chuck agreed. "When I was in the seventh grade, I think we won only two games and one was from a forfeit. The other team's bus broke down, and they couldn't make it to the field. Their coach wasn't able to reschedule, so we got the win. I think that was my best game!" He patted his trophy, then put it back up on the shelf.

"Keep going, Chuck — this is great stuff! You're on a roll!" Dan said.

"But what about me?" Koby interrupted. "I didn't finish what I had to say about Chuck's influence on me."

"We'll get back to you, Koby," Dan answered. "Just sit tight."

So Koby sat back and let Chuck do most of the talking. Almost all of what he said had to do with teamwork, sportsmanship, and playing one's hardest for the sake of the common goal.

"Winning?" Dan guessed.

Chuck gave a meaningful smile. "No. The common goal was to leave the field satisfied that we'd played our best and helped our teammates play their best, too. At the end of the day, we couldn't have done any better than that. I think that's why, unlike a lot of losing teams, no one on our squad ever got on anyone else's case. We were a tight-knit, loyal bunch," he concluded, "and that's why that trophy means so much to me."

After the interview, at Mrs. Caplin's request, Dan and Buck stayed for dinner.

"That was a mighty fine meal," Buck said. "It was better than a four-star restaurant."

"Mmmm, it just stuck to my ribs," Dan added. "I better move my belt buckle over a notch or two. But now we should get to the station for an editing session. Before we go, though, Koby, I want to get a few shots of you and your brother playing some catch in the driveway, if that's OK."

"Fine with me," Koby's mother said, "as long as Koby and Chuck can help me clean up here first."

"We'll help, too," Buck volunteered. "C'mon, Dan, prove to everyone here that Channel 5 has manners."

"I'm on it," Dan said with a smile. "Big appetites and manners — that's us!"

They all helped to clean up and do the dishes. When everything was done, Koby went to the back porch to get two gloves and a ball while Dan and Buck set up in the driveway.

The camera began rolling again.

"Hey, Chuck, let's go into the driveway and play some catch, you know, like the olden days when you were a lot younger," Koby said with a smirk.

"I still don't think you can catch my fastball," Chuck answered. "You never could!"

"Just watch!"

Chuck went into an exaggerated windup and unleashed a fastball.

Phwap!

"Pretty good, big brother, pretty good!" Koby yelled as he pretended to fall back from the impact.

"Now let me see yours, little brother. Just 'chuck' it over!"

" 'Chuck' it, huh? No prob, fasten your seat belt!" Koby said. He imitated Chuck's delivery exactly and sent a smoker down the middle of the strike zone.

Phwap!

"Ow!" Chuck cried. "That pitch is a lethal weapon. Now I can understand why you're having such a great year."

Koby grinned. "Yeah, thanks to pitches like that, Monticello should win the Meadowbrook Conference. I must say, it's been a long time coming. I'm just glad I was able to turn this team around and give Monticello a winning season for once. The team just needed a superstar like me to light a fire under them, that's all!"

Chuck balked in mid-throw and stared open-mouthed at his brother.

Koby laughed. "What's the matter, Chuck? Forget how to pitch?"

Chuck slowly shook his head. "No. But I think you're forgetting something."

Koby looked mystified. "What're you talking about?"

"If you have to ask, then I doubt you'll figure it out. But maybe you will. Hopefully you will. And in time to be the player I think you are."

With that, he took off his glove and returned to the house. Koby started after him, then saw that the camera was still on. So instead, he picked up the ball that had rolled out of Chuck's glove and tossed it up in the air a few times. He cracked a weak smile and said, "Just practicing fielding pop flies."

But after a few more tosses, Buck clicked the camera off and signaled to Dan that they were done for the day.

The Megaphone

Monticello Middle School
June 3

SPORTS SHORTS

by Sara Wilson

You've probably all heard by now that our flying-high Cardinals took a bit of a nosedive in their rematch against the Greenview Green Jackets. Pitcher Koby Caplin slipped, allowing four hits and an unusual number of balls. The Green Jackets walked away from Cain Park Field with a solid 3–1 victory.

This defeat doesn't hurt the Cardinals, as they maintain their one game lead over the Danville Mudcats, but it does bruise the team ego.

But here's an alarming bit of information a

secret source passed on to me. According to my informant, at least one error—an error that eventually led to a run being scored, mind you — might have been avoided. It seems our own TV celebrity, Koby Caplin, refused to throw the pitches his battery mate, Tug McCue, signaled for. In fact, he started choosing his own pitches. Would Tug have been able to nab the strike that got by him if he'd known what to look for? No one will ever know... but in the meantime, the Cardinals chalked up their first loss.

Ah, well. We can only hope that Koby will remember what teamwork is before the game against Runkle. (But maybe he's lost himself to stardom completely?)

Miguel Sanchez will be on the mound for Monticello versus the Erieview Jethawks, so be there if you can to cheer him on!

"Sports Shorts" Trivia Question: Which major league team once wore shorts for its uniform?

Answer to the last trivia question: Houston Astro Bob Watson scored the millionth run in major league history on May 4, 1975, at Candlestick Park, in San Francisco. He scored from second base on a three-run homer by teammate Milt May at 12:32 in the afternoon.

Koby's heart sank as he read Sara's article. He was glad Dan and Buck weren't around with the camera. He wasn't sure he could control the panicked look on his face.

How could she have written that about me? he wondered. And how did she learn about the signals? There's only one person who could have told her, he figured: Tug.

Koby recalled seeing the two of them with their heads together right after the Greenview game. He flushed — but whether from a sense of betrayal or guilt at having been found out, he didn't ask himself. All he knew was that he had to find Sara and hear for himself that Tug had been the source.

But when he tracked Sara down just before lunch, she was tight-lipped.

"My source asked not to be identified" was all she would say. "But I will tell you this. It wasn't who you think. It wasn't Tug."

Koby snorted. "Oh, come off it, Sara. Stop trying to make the Cardinals into some kind of mystery, with villains and heroes and intrigue, just so people will keep reading the *Megaphone*. I thought you were a better reporter than that."

Sara's eyes blazed. "Seems to me you didn't question my reporting abilities when I had nice things to say about you," she retorted. "Funny how I don't hear you denying that your actions led to Tug's error and a run for the opposite team. Tell me, Koby, would you be confronting me if, instead of fingering you as the problem, I'd said it was Tug? Would you have come here and defended him by admitting that it might have been your fault?"

Koby was silent.

"I thought so. And as for revealing my source, forget it. Now, if you'll excuse me, I'd like to go to lunch. Although my appetite isn't what it was a few minutes ago." She pushed by him and stalked into the cafeteria.

Koby had no choice but to follow her. He picked up a tray and loaded it down with food, then headed for his usual table, where Tug, K.O., Scoop, and Prez were already sitting. On the table in front of them was a copy of the *Megaphone*.

Nobody moved when he tried to squeeze in.

"Hey, you guys, can you make some room?" Koby asked.

Scoop, K.O., and Prez gave him hostile glares in

response. Tug didn't even look up. Then Prez said, "This table's reserved for *team* players. No room for hotshots who gamble with the team's record for personal glory."

Koby flushed. "Fine, I'll go somewhere else. But before I do — Tug, can I ask you something?"

Tug stared at his tray and said, "Yeah, what is it?"

"Sara said you weren't the one who told her about my calling my own pitches. Is that right?"

Tug's head snapped up. "If that's what she told you, why would you think she was lying? Jeez, Koby, you're really turning into a jerk, you know that?"

Now it was Koby's turn to stare at his tray. He knew Tug was right, that he was accusing Sara of being deceitful. But Tug still hadn't answered his question. And despite what Sara had said, Koby needed to hear it from Tug himself.

Tug seemed to realize this, too. He blew out his breath and said, "We've always had great teamwork, but now, just because of that stupid TV show, you decide you don't need me." Tug shook his head. "The difference between you and me, Koby, is that I still believe our pitcher-catcher relationship can work. I wouldn't do anything to mess that up. And that includes going to the *Megaphone* behind your back! So I guess you'll just have to keep looking for the 'secret source,' 'cuz you ain't lookin' at him right now."

With that, Tug picked up his tray and left the table. Scoop, Prez, and K.O. followed, leaving Koby to sit alone and eat his cold lunch.

Practice was awful for Koby. No one talked to him except to warn him when a ball was coming his way. When it was over, he walked home by himself, miserable.

After his shower, he got a piece of news that brightened him up a bit. His mother told him that Dan had called from the station. "He said if you want to come down to look at the film footage Buck's taken already, you're welcome to. Sounds like that could be interesting."

Chuck looked up from the table where he'd been reading the newspaper. "It does sound interesting," he said. "In fact, I'd like to tag along if that's OK with you."

Koby nodded happily. He called Dan back to say they were on their way.

Fifteen minutes later, Koby, Buck, Dan, and Chuck were gathered around a TV monitor. Buck loaded in a cassette and started the machine running.

Clip after clip of Koby danced by on the screen. But after the first minute, Koby barely even looked at himself. He was too busy listening to what he had said. And what he heard caused him to shrink into his seat.

" 'Thanks to pitches like that, Monticello should win the Meadowbrook Conference. . . .' "

" 'But what about me? I didn't finish what I had to say about Chuck's influence on me. . . .' "

" 'The team just needed a superstar like me to light a fire under them. . . .' "

When the video ended, Koby couldn't look at any of the others. Chuck broke the silence.

"Well, that sure is something."

Koby finally looked up. His voice was thick. "I didn't know I'd been such a jerk. No wonder Tug and Sara hate me. And now the team does, too."

Chuck put his arm around Koby's shoulder and gave him a squeeze. "Koby, I know you feel lousy right now. And you should. But it's not too late to make things right. Is it, Dan?"

Koby looked at Dan hopefully.

Dan nodded. "I think we can work on it." Koby's face brightened. "No promises, though," Dan added. "We're under a tight schedule. Anything we do will have to be done quickly. We'll have to use some of this footage. Otherwise, we won't have enough to fill the whole documentary."

"But what if we made some new footage?" Koby asked.

Dan drummed his fingers on the table. "We'll be shooting the game against Runkle, but that's cutting it pretty close. We'll try, though, but like I said: No promises."

12

The atmosphere in the locker room was charged up before the game against Runkle.

Koby sat alone on the bench in front of his locker. He pounded the pocket in his mitt as he looked down at the floor.

I'll just show these guys on the field what I'm made of, he said to himself.

"OK, men, listen up!" Coach Tomashiro said as he gathered his troops.

Koby found a space at the edge of the circle.

"Win or lose, we can all hold our heads up high when the season ends this afternoon. A win over the Firebirds, as you know, will clinch the Meadowbrook Conference title, something we haven't accomplished in many years. Yeah, a conference championship award would look mighty fine in our trophy case. But you know what I think will look — and feel — even better is if you play your hearts out! That's something you can always carry with you. So come on, everyone put your hands in the middle...."

Each member of the team put a hand on top of the next guy's. "GO, CARDINALS!"

"EEEEOOOOO!" the team yelled and jumped as they ran behind the coach.

"Cardinals! Cardinals!" The full house exploded with chants as they spotted the team trotting onto the field. "We're number one! We're number one!"

It was an SRO crowd again.

Koby caught up with Tug. "Hey, Tug, want to warm up?"

Tug didn't say anything at first. He looked around the field and saw that Coach Tomashiro was staring right at him.

"Yeah, sure, Koby. Um, uh, I've got to get the Hummer first. I'll meet you over at the backstop."

As Tug walked off, Koby approached Coach Tomashiro. "Coach? Uh, I want you to know that

I'm sorry about the way I've been acting lately. I've been a real loser. I'm kind of surprised you even kept me on the mound. I know how strongly you feel about 'prized bears.'"

Coach Tomashiro regarded Koby silently for a moment, then laid a hand on his shoulder. "Koby, I was against doing this TV show from the beginning, even though I knew it could help bring fans to the stands. But I wanted to put a stop to the whole thing when I saw what it was turning you into. I kept my mouth shut, though, because I needed to know you could find your way back by yourself. I'm very glad you did."

"Thanks, Coach," Koby said with a small smile. Coach T. returned the smile, then sent Koby over to the backstop, where Tug was waiting.

"Ready to catch some pitches, Tug?"

"We've got to get ready for the game, don't we?" Tug said matter-of-factly.

Koby threw his routine of warm-up pitches.

And Tug caught them.

In dead silence.

When the umpire called for the game to begin,

Koby couldn't let the silence continue. He had to say at least one thing to Tug.

"You signal; I'll throw," he said simply.

Tug glanced at him and, after a beat, nodded slowly.

"OK, team, everyone on the bench!" Coach Tomashiro yelled. "Everyone's hands in the middle for the last time this season!" he said as he looked every player in the eye. "Together: GO, CARDINALS!"

"GO, CARDINALS!" the team yelled.

"Now, get to your positions! The game is going to start."

"PLAY BALL!" the umpire roared.

Koby trotted to the pitcher's mound and stooped to pick up the rosin. He scanned the crowd and saw Sara, his parents, and his teachers sitting nearby. He spotted Dan and Buck, too. Buck's camera was at his shoulder, ready to capture the action.

OK, this is your chance to make things right, Koby reminded himself.

Koby had to battle not only the Runkle School artillery but ninety-degree heat as well. He went into his trademark high-kick windup and unleashed a sizzling fastball high and outside to the first Firebird at the plate. The crowd rallied behind the first pitch.

"Ball one!" shouted the umpire.

Koby's teammates were silent behind him. "Hey, this isn't a funeral, you guys! Talk it up!" yelled Coach Tomashiro.

The defense perked up. But knowing they were cheering for him only because the coach had ordered them to made Koby feel awful. He suddenly realized how much he depended on their support.

He walked the batter on four straight pitches.

The next batter sliced Koby's fastball up the middle. Sandy dove to his right, but the ball beat his outstretched hand.

The Firebird fans went wild.

Runners at first and second. Sweat poured from Koby's forehead as he rubbed his face on his sleeve.

He threw his next pitch into the dirt. Tug managed to recover it, then asked for time and walked the ball to the mound.

Tug handed the ball to Koby and said,

"Remember, this is for the team championship of the conference."

Koby said in a soft voice, "I know. Believe me, Tug, I know." He caught Tug's eyes for an instant. He wasn't sure, but he thought he saw a spark of their former friendship light up in them. Then Tug turned his back and headed for home plate.

With renewed intensity, Koby buckled down, but he couldn't find the strike zone. Working to a 3 and 1 count, the batter took his chances and watched the next pitch go by for ball four.

The Cardinals fans were silenced, and Koby's teammates were stunned.

Suddenly a voice called out. "C'mon, Kobe! You can do it!" It was Tug.

Scoop's big voice followed moments later. "Come on, Kobe! You got what it takes!"

"You got it, man!" Billy added. "This is Cardinals ball we're playing!"

The rest of the team joined in the chatter.

With bases loaded, the Firebird batter was looking at a chance to score some runs.

Koby dug his cleat into the dirt and kicked at the

pitcher's mound. Taking a deep breath, he bore down and threw a smoker.

Phwap!

The Hummer hugged the ball as the batter got nothing but air.

The next pitch was foul-tipped to the backstop.

The batter was in the hole with an 0–2 count. As he let loose his third pitch, Koby felt like he was getting back in control.

The batter swung for more air. Strike three! Suddenly the stands came alive.

"Ko-by!" rocked the fans. "Ko-by!"

The next batter hit a dribbler back to Koby. Koby checked the runner at third and then threw to Prez at first. Prez snagged the throw seconds before the batter crossed the base. Out number two.

The next Firebird hit a routine fly to Beechie in center, and the side was retired in order.

Beechie led off the Cardinals' offensive attack with a double to right. Koby followed with a walk, and K.O. connected for a double, scoring Beechie and sending Koby to third. Tug popped out to second, but Koby tagged up and crossed home plate.

Then Scoop singled, but the first baseman nabbed K.O. at third.

"Nice try, K.O.!" Coach T. yelled. "We'll get 'em next time!"

Prez grounded out to third to end the inning.

Two runs, three hits, and one runner left.

Going into the second inning with a two-run lead helped the team find its full voice. Though they weren't yelling specifically for him, their enthusiasm fired up Koby's confidence.

Koby retired the first two batters he faced.

Next up was Sammy Transom, Koby's opposing pitcher and an excellent scratch hitter. Sammy crouched down so low that the strike zone seemed smaller than a bread box.

Koby went to work.

He threw a low and inside pitch that Sammy pulled down the third base line for a base hit. The next batter hit a line drive right into Prez's waiting glove. The inning ended with Sammy stranded at first.

At the end of three innings, the Cardinals still held on to their two-run lead.

In the top of the fourth, the first Firebird up punched a one-hopper to right for a base hit.

Next up was Sammy. Koby tossed him a series of low and inside sidearm pitches that Sammy lunged at like a blindfolded child going after a piñata. But Koby had his number, and Sammy went down swinging.

The next batter, Skip Wright, singled to left, sending the runner to third. Runners on first and third. The next batter hit a slashing ground ball to Papo, who flipped it to Sandy at second for the out.

But the runner at third scored on the play, and the Firebirds went on board with their first run.

Koby got the next batter to fly out to Beechie to retire the side. Score: Cardinals 2, Firebirds 1.

In the bottom of the fourth, Papo and Billy started the inning with pop fly outs to short center. Sandy and Beechie countered with back-to-back singles. With runners on first and second and nobody out, Koby stepped up to the plate. Sammy had a score to settle since Koby had fanned him the last time out.

Koby looked at the first two pitches — one ball and one strike.

Sandy took a big lead off second, and Sammy

went for the pickoff. Sandy dove into the bag for a sand sandwich.

"Safe!" the umpire shouted.

Koby suppressed a grin. Thanks, Sandy, he thought. I appreciate you rattling our friend Sammy out there!

Sammy threw a fastball, and Koby went after it, shooting for the stars.

Nothing.

The count was 1 and 2.

Sandy and Beechie were ready to fly.

Koby stepped out of the batter's box.

"Time!" yelled the ump.

Koby tapped his cleats with the bat. He checked out the bench. Coach Tomashiro was standing there with his arms crossed in front of his chest. Then Koby spotted Sara in the stands. She stopped writing and returned his stare.

The quiet of the moment turned to a chorus of cheers as the Cardinals fans chanted, "Ko-by!"

Koby stepped back into the box. Sammy threw a fastball as Koby pulled his bat as far back as he could, feeling his muscles stretch. The ball seemed to travel in slow motion as it crossed the plate.

Crack!

Koby slammed a solid single over the shortstop's head and loaded the bases.

The fans were cheering, but they weren't yelling for Koby. The name they were calling was K.O., who strode to the plate. Koby knew he was hoping to send at least one of his teammates home.

He didn't. He popped out to end the inning.

Disappointment written all over his face, K.O. dropped the bat and removed his batting helmet.

Koby jogged in. He was disappointed, too, but he didn't want K.O. to feel any worse.

"That's OK, K.O.!" he cried. The cheer was taken up by the rest of the Cardinals. Soon the fans were yelling it, too.

"That's OK, K.O.! That's OK, K.O.!"

K.O. finally cracked a smile and headed out to his position.

As he passed Koby, he stuck out his hand and said, "Thanks, man."

Koby grinned and slapped K.O.'s palm. "That's what teammates are for."

13

The Cardinals held on to their 2–1 lead into the top of the sixth.

One more inning till the Meadowbrook Championship is ours! Koby thought excitedly.

The first Firebird batter popped a high fly ball that Prez snagged at first. With one down, the next batter up hit a hard bouncer over the second base bag just out of Sandy's reach.

The runner challenged Koby at first by taking a big lead. Koby looked him back, but the runner was off once Koby committed to his pitch.

Tug was ready. He threw a bullet from his crouching position. Sandy was in place as the runner dove headfirst into the second base bag.

"Out!" shouted the umpire.

Koby gave Tug and Sandy a thumbs-up.

"TUG! SANDY!" rallied the crowd.

With two down, the batter outran a hard-hit grounder. Runner on first, and Sammy was up at the plate.

Koby looked at Tug's signals. He nodded and threw an off-speed pitch that kissed the inside corner.

"Strike one!" yelled the ump.

Sammy readied himself for the next pitch.

Koby went back to the inside, but the pitch was right at the numbers. Sammy punched it over the outstretched hands of Scoop in left field. Two runs scored as the runner and Sammy both crossed the plate.

Firebirds 3, Cardinals 2.

"Maybe he wants it more than you!" a fan yelled at Koby.

Koby nervously touched the brim of his cap as he stood on the mound.

"You'll get the next guy!" Tug yelled.

"Yeah, no prob!" shouted Billy.

"This game is ours!" Papo joined in.

"This game is *ours!*" Prez echoed. "We can do it!"

"Let's go, Koby! You're our man!" barked K.O.

The whole Cardinals squad joined in the chatter. Koby's heart soared. He faced the next Firebird hitter with a steely look of determination.

Three straight pitches, and the batter went down swinging for the third out.

The team hustled in from the field, eager to get their last ups.

"Wait for your pitch, Cardinals!" ordered Coach Tomashiro. "Let the pitcher pitch to you."

Beechie led off with a dribbler right back to the pitcher. He sped down the first base line, but Sammy threw him out by half a step.

Next up: Koby. The fans were on their feet.

Koby stepped into the box with a resolute look on his face.

Sammy threw him a speeder down the middle, and Koby scratched out a base hit into short right.

The crowd and his team were with him all the way.

K.O. followed with a line out to short. Koby took a few steps but stayed on first.

Two outs, one man on.

Tug walked up to the plate.

"C'mon, Tug, you can do it, you can do it!" Koby hollered. The stands took up the cheer.

Sammy worked a 2–2 count. Tug took the next pitch and fouled it off the backstop.

He stepped out of the batter's box, ran his hands up and down the bat, then stepped back in. The fans were roaring, but now Koby was silent. With all his mental strength, he willed Tug to make a hit.

Sammy bore down and threw the next pitch with everything he had.

Crack!

Tug connected for a tape-measure homer that sailed over the left-field fence!

The Cardinals won the game and the Meadowbrook Conference!

"Yahoooo!" roared the crowd. "TUG! KOBY! CARDINALS! CARDINALS!"

As the bench cleared to welcome Koby and Tug to home plate, Coach Tomashiro bear-hugged every player in sight.

Dan and Buck raced to the plate to catch the excitement on film. Koby and Tug were buried in a pileup. Buck kneeled on the ground to get a good shot of Koby.

Koby yelled loudly and clearly into the camera, "I'm not the story — the Cardinals are!" He pointed to the mass of knees and elbows all around him.

Dan offered his hand, "Here, Koby, let me help you up!" He pulled a happily grinning Koby free from the pileup.

"Thanks, Dan. I felt like a sardine down there!"

Dan ushered Koby away from the crowd.

"Koby, I hate to pull you away from the celebration, but if we're going to get to the studio to look through the new material, we don't have any time to waste."

Koby nodded quickly. "I've got some ideas about some other stuff we can do, Dan. Is that OK?"

"Why don't you explain it to me on the ride over?" Dan turned to his cameraman. "Buck, hand me the tape from your camera, and you can use a fresh one to finish up here. As soon as you're done here, race back to the station!"

"OK, chief!" Buck said with a smile. "But before I forget, Kobe, good going, man! You guys are really champs!"

"Thanks, Buck, I really appre —"

"Hey, you guys, don't get sentimental on me! We've got a job to do," Dan said as he nudged Koby along through the crowd.

14

Dan and Koby pulled into the Channel 5 side lot and parked the van. They hurried into the station but were stopped by a security guard behind a giant counter.

"Hey, Dan, where's the fire?" the security guard asked.

"I've got a deadline, Fred," Dan said. "Koby, here, is with me."

"OK. He'll have to sign in, and then I'll buzz you both through."

Koby dashed off his signature and followed Dan down a long hallway. When they reached the stairway, Dan pushed open the heavy metal door and took the steps two at a time. Koby tried to keep up with him.

"Here we are!" Dan said as he pushed open a black door. "This is the editing room. First thing we are going to do is work on making a new promo. I'm going to load today's tape into the editing system. Look at the viewer, and we can decide if we can use anything from today's shooting. Then we'll finish up the documentary."

"Gotcha!" Koby said enthusiastically.

"This new promo has to be ready to air during tonight's six o'clock news."

"OK, chief," Koby said with a big smile, enjoying his role as a video assistant. "And Dan, I want to thank you for doing all this for me."

"Now, I already told you not to get all sentimental on me. Remember, I'm a hard-nosed TV producer. Anyway, I think I need to be thanking *you* for reminding me what's really important about playing sports. As soon as Buck gets here we'll — speaking of the devil!"

"OK, guys, here's the rest of today's action," Buck said as he flung open the door. "I got some good shots of the postgame celebration, and I think there are a few good sound bites that we can use for the promo."

"Good," said Dan. "Now, let's get busy, because we're going to have to go into overdrive to get everything done. It's four-thirty, so that gives us an hour or so to put something together."

Together, Dan, Buck, and Koby reviewed footage from the game.

"Wait! Stop!" Koby cried. "That's the bit I want you to use." Dan stopped the tape, rewound it, and played the segment again.

He glanced at Buck, then asked Koby if he was sure.

"Positive."

Dan grinned. "OK, then. It works for me. Now, we'll add some music underneath, and then we'll have to redub the narration. I can handle that part. Buck, take Koby into a studio and get a camera on him. Koby has one last thing he wants to add to the documentary. If it works out OK, we'll use it. But Koby, if it doesn't, we'll have to use what we've got already. OK?"

Koby nodded. "But don't worry. I know it will work out."

Buck stood up. "Well, it will only work out if we

make it — and we're running out of time! So let's move."

Buck ushered Koby into a studio and sat him on a chair near a microphone. He fiddled with some lights, then adjusted a camera until it was pointing right at Koby.

All the while, Koby quietly rehearsed what he wanted to say.

Finally, Buck told him they were ready to begin. "When I say go, you say your piece," Buck called as he disappeared into the equipment area. "OK, ready? Go."

Koby looked directly into the camera. He took a deep breath, then started talking.

Three minutes later, he was done.

Buck hurried out. "Nice job, Koby."

Koby looked up at him. "You think so?"

Buck patted him on the shoulder. "Definitely. I wouldn't change a thing. You really got to the heart of the matter — and professionally speaking, you looked and sounded good doing it. Ever think of doing this sort of thing for a living?"

Koby cracked a grin. "Maybe someday. But right

now, I've had just about enough of being in the spotlight!"

Dan stuck his head in the door. "Good, you guys are done. Koby, your dad called. He'll be here in a few minutes to pick you up. You'll probably get home just in time to see the promo air."

"I can't wait to see it!"

When Mr. Caplin phoned up from the security desk, Buck walked Koby downstairs.

"You've got a lot to be proud of today, Mr. Caplin," Buck said to Koby's dad.

"I sure do." Mr. Caplin ruffled his hand through Koby's hair. "You know, son, your mom and I didn't even get a chance to congratulate you after the game this afternoon. When Dan phoned yesterday to say that he'd be taking you to the studio right after the game, I now see he really meant *right* after the game! You were gone like a flash!"

"Well, we had a job to do that was even more important than the game!" Koby said.

"We'll have the final documentary finished by tomorrow," Buck said, "and ready to air for prime time — Friday night at eight! I have a sneaking sus- picion your family will be watching it."

"Yeah, and I'm going to be sure to make a copy and send it to Chuck!"

Buck winked at him, then disappeared back into the station.

Mr. Caplin looked at Koby quizzically. "What was that all about?"

"You'll see." Koby smiled mysteriously.

When Koby and his dad pulled in the driveway, Mrs. Caplin rushed out to greet them. "Welcome home, champ!"

"Thanks, Mom," Koby said. "C'mon, you guys. It's five to six, and Dan said the new promo's gonna run during the six o'clock news. I'll get the VCR ready."

His parents hurried in after him. They gathered in the living room.

"Dad picked up some pizza earlier for the special event. I'll heat it up," Mrs. Caplin said.

Koby put a cassette in the VCR and flicked on the television just in time. The promo started with the end of the game against the Firebirds. Dan's voiceover announced the Cardinals' victory over Runkle and their championship status. He went on to say that Channel 5 was proud to present a profile of one of the team's key players.

The camera closed in on Koby. He was pointing to his teammates and saying, "I'm not the story, the Cardinals are!"

"Well done!" Koby's dad said.

"I'm proud of you, Koby," his mom added. "Very proud!"

"Thanks, Mom!" Koby said with a grin. "Now, how about that pizza?"

Koby scarfed down a few slices, then sat back.

"That was delicious," he said. "Can I go outside and throw the ball against the pitch-back? I'm a little too pumped up to start on my homework!"

"Go right ahead. You've earned it," his mom said.

Koby grabbed his mitt and a ball and headed out the door to the driveway. He got the pitch-back out of the garage and set it up at the end of the driveway in front of the garage door.

Koby threw a mixture of overhand fastballs and sidearm off-speed pitches. For the first time in weeks, he found he was concentrating solely on pitching. Not on where the camera was. Not on what he was going to say. And not on who else was talking or writing about him. It felt great.

"Hey, Kobe!" somebody yelled as Koby went into his windup.

Koby turned around to see who it was.

"Hey, Tug!" he said with a startled look on his face.

"I was watching the six o'clock news with my mom when the promo came on for the documentary. I just wanted to tell you I thought it was pretty cool." Tug extended his hand to Koby.

Koby shook it. "Do you want to come over and watch the documentary with us tomorrow night?"

Tug broke into a huge grin. "I wouldn't miss a chance to see myself on camera — even if it is as a second banana to you!"

The Megaphone

Monticello Middle School
June 17

SPORTS SHORTS
by Sara Wilson

When I looked in my sportswriter crystal ball at the beginning of the season, I saw some improvement, perhaps, and a bit of the ol' Monticello pride returning. But a championship — hardly!

I remember asking Coach T. for his thoughts about the upcoming season. He said that Monticello has had a string of rough seasons but that's behind them. "You can't steal second if you keep your foot on first."

Well, we not only stole second — we took the whole diamond!

I'm not going to take space here to recap the final game against the Runkle School Firebirds, but in case you missed the action, the final score of Thursday's game was Monticello 4, Firebirds 3.

I'm not going to mention any players by name because every player on the team is a champ.

You see, today's column is really just a thank-you note to the Cardinals and to Coach T., because the biggest winners were the fans.

This was a season designed for prime time. Thanks for the memories.

This is Sara Wilson, signing off till September.

(Remember, you have one more chance to relive the memory: Check out the Channel 5 documentary Friday night at eight.)

"Sports Shorts" Trivia Question: (Here's an easy one to end the school year. If you can't guess the answer, look for it in next year's first edition of the *Megaphone*!) What team, at the beginning of the season, was the most unlikely candidate to win the Meadowbrook Junior High Conference title?

Answer to the last trivia question: In 1976, the Chicago White Sox experimented with knee-length pants — but quickly switched back to long pants. (Imagine how it felt to slide in shorts!)

---

*　❋　❋*

Friday night at five of eight.

Koby's dad pushed some additional chairs into the living room so there would be a seat for everyone they had invited.

"Is there any more popcorn?" Tug asked.

"Yeah, I'll get it. You're really a bottomless pit tonight, Tug," Koby said as he ran into the kitchen.

"Hey, Kobe, hurry up! It's starting," Sara yelled.

Koby ran through the kitchen door, balancing a bowl of popcorn and some sodas. "Dad, can you flip in the cassette, please. I want a copy of this!"

The program started with a voiceover of Dan: "What you are about to see is the hard work and triumphs of a middle school athletic team — the Monticello Middle School Cardinals — as they embark on a sports adventure that will take them to the top of the Meadowbrook Conference."

"Wow, is he talking about us?" Koby said with a laugh. "It sounds so official!"

"Yeah, it sounds very 'newsy.'" Tug chipped in. "I wouldn't even know it was Dan's voice."

Dan continued: "We will look at the season through the eyes of a determined and dedicated right-handed pitcher, Koby Caplin..."

"He's making you sound pretty good!" Tug said as he threw a pillow at Koby.

"Yeah, you can do all kinds of tricks with television! Shhh, I want to hear this next part!" Koby said as he threw the pillow back at Tug.

They all watched as the video showed highlights from the season.

"...and hear in Koby Caplin's own words about what made the Cardinals into a championship team."

Koby's voice continued as the voiceover: "There are no prized bears on the Monticello Cardinals. That's what Coach T. would tell the team every day —"

"Hey, Kobe, Coach T. will like that you quoted him. It might help with your social studies grade!"

"Cut it out, man, and listen! This next part I want to see!"

The camera panned Chuck's room, ending with a close-up of the Team Spirit Award on the shelf.

Koby continued: "...and this is what every player

should work toward, whether you actually get the trophy or not. The real award is trying your hardest and doing all that you can do to work together as a team. My brother, Chuck, taught me that. And if he's watching now, Chuck, I want you to know I got your message. And Sara didn't even have to reveal you as her 'secret source.' "

Sara shot Koby a smile over her shoulder. Koby gave her a thumbs-up, then turned his attention back to the screen.

"Sometimes it's easy to lose sight of the real goal. You can get too bogged down comparing stats, or looking for your name in the paper, or trying to win games single-handedly. I ought to know. It happened to me while this documentary was being filmed."

Koby glanced around the room at his friends and family. Each of them had a smile on his or her face.

"But middle school team athletics aren't about the individual. They're about learning to be a part of the whole, building friendships, and reaching together for the prize. Well, the Cardinals won the prize this year — and I'm happy that I was able to be a part of it all. GO, CARDINALS!"

Epilogue

Applause filled the room as Principal Sleeper introduced the team at the baseball awards banquet. As each player was called up, he handed him a championship certificate and a small trophy.

Coach Tomashiro stepped up to the podium to hand out the two major awards. The cafeteria got very quiet.

"Let me first say that I am proud of every player up here. I'm also proud and very appreciative of all of you out there who supported us this season. There are two awards that give me a great sense of honor to present. The first is for the Most Valuable Player of the Meadowbrook Conference, as voted on by all the coaches in the league. I am pleased to present this trophy to our own Koby Caplin."

Everyone jumped to their feet and applauded. "Koby, could you please come forward to accept this trophy?"

Koby stood from his seat and walked up to the stage. Coach Tomashiro shook his hand and handed him the trophy.

"Thanks, Coach!" Koby said above the roar of the crowd. He stood quietly as Coach Tomashiro began his next presentation.

"And it is my equal pleasure and honor to present this next trophy for the Team Spirit Award. Tug McCue, would you please step forward!"

Tug leaped onto the stage two steps at a time, then took his place next to Koby.

"Hey, shove over — you're in my light," Koby whispered to his pal. Tug gave him a sidelong glance and met Koby's grin. The boys' laughter mingled with the sound of applause. Each with an arm around the other's shoulders, they held their trophies aloft and gave a whoop.

Matt Christopher

Sports Bio Bookshelf

Michael Jordan

Steve Young

Grant Hill

Wayne Gretzky

Greg Maddux

Ken Griffey Jr.

Andre Agassi

Mo Vaughn

Emmitt Smith

Hakeem Olajuwon

Tiger Woods

Randy Johnson

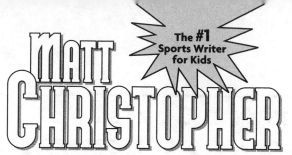

The #1 Sports Writer for Kids

Read them all!

All available in paperback from Little, Brown and Company

Join the Matt Christopher Fan Club!

To get your official membership card, the Matt Christopher
Sports Pages, and a handy bookmark, send a business-size
(9$^{1}/_{2}$" x 4") self-addressed, stamped envelope and
$1.00 (in cash or a check payable to
Little, Brown and Company) to:

Matt Christopher Fan Club
c/o Little, Brown and Company
3 Center Plaza
Boston, MA 02108